MW01221789

This novel contains scenes of terror, heavy violence, gore, coarse language, and disturbing themes some readers may find offensive. Discretion is advised.

Copyright © 2021 By Andrew McManaman

Book design by Meg Rhoads

ISBN 978-1-7778059-0-6 (paperback)
ISBN 978-1-7778059-1-3 (ebook)

popcornpaperbacks.com

For my parents, thank you for everything.

AND NOW, A FEATURE
PRESENTATION FOR YOUR
IMAGINATION!

DOLLHOUSE

Popcorn
Paperbacks

Whose woods these are I think I know.
His house is in the village though;
He will not see me stopping here
To watch his woods fill up with snow.

My little horse must think it queer
To stop without a farmhouse near
Between the woods and frozen lake
The darkest evening of the year.

He gives his harness bells a shake
To ask if there is some mistake.
The only other sound's the sweep
Of easy winds and downy flake.

The woods are lovely dark and deep.
But I have promises to keep,
And miles to go before I sleep,
And miles to go before I sleep.
-Robert Frost

ACT I

1

The distant thunderclap cut like a knife. Snapping her eyelids back, Darla awoke from the deepest sleep she could recall. The fog in her mind kept things from being clear. Gripping the pillow, she squeezed it, listening—the room was barely visible, light cast from behind her. Her thoughts began to race about what that clatter could have been. As her eyes adjusted, Darla saw the room she was in, and it wasn't hers. Rolling onto her back, she scanned the room—no recognition of the ceiling, the blue walls, or the bed she lay in.

BANG!

The same clatter brought Darla lurching upwards, clasping her gray knitted cardigan with her left hand against her chest. Her eyes were wide and terrified. Turning to her left, she saw a window allowing in the natural sunlight, nearly blinding her. Predictable questions ran through her mind. *What's going on? Where am I? How'd I get—"*

Muffled voices abruptly rose from outside her bedroom door. Darla snapped her eyes and attention towards it, listening in. She couldn't quite make out what it was—the voices were unfamiliar. A fiery yell barrelled from outside her room, followed by:

BANG!

The sound of the impact resonated in her chest, making her stomach jump. Her eyes finally adjusted to the light in the room. Darla peeked outside the small bedroom window. She was in a house surrounded by dark trees stretching as far as her eyes could see. Her heart was beating double-time— her breathing, rapid. Taking her feet off the bed and resting them on the cold wooden floor, the edge of her right foot nudged her shoes placed neatly side by side. Slipping them on, she made her way to the door.

BANG!

Again, it roared. Darla tiptoed over, leaned in, and pressed her ear against the door. The muffled voices still spoke. From what she could gather, it was two men. "My captives?" Darla questioned. Pondering, she tried to think of her last memory. The vision of her children, Luke and Olivia, brushing their teeth came to mind. But that was it. Nothing equalled her waking in this bed, in this room, in this house. A debate raged in her mind: Should I or should I not go out there?

Darla retraced her steps. She went around to the opposite side of the bed and the window. Looking for a way to open it, to her surprise, she found none. The window was just that—a window. It had no handle to grab onto to slide it open. Pushing it also proved useless. The windows were not made to be opened.

Another clatter broke out, followed by, "FUCK!" from one of the men. Taking a breath, Darla made her way back to the door. She leaned in again, trying to make out what the two men were doing. The debate no longer raged in her mind. One answer stood clear as victor.

Taking a deep breath, Darla grasped the knob of the bedroom door. Twisting it, she pulled it open a sliver. Light washed over Darla. Peeking her head through the gap, she saw a hallway full of doors, all white with black numbers hanging in the middle. Darla caught the number on her door as she turned and gazed up. Room 5.

"Fuckin' hell!" she heard.

Darla's gaze followed the hallway to an open concept living room with two men—one tall and one short—standing side by side. The taller stranger held a black stool in his hands, both hands clasped tightly around the legs. The shorter man had his arms crossed as he stared out the window. Squinting, she tried to see what they were viewing. From what she could gather, it was just more trees on that side too. The taller man then lifted the stool like he was the next batter up. From hip to above his shoulders, the man held it high and ready to swing. Then, taking three great strides toward the window, he swung the stool, and it collided with the left of the two windows in the living room. The window did not shatter. In fact, it seemed as though the window had spat the stool back.

The taller man lowered the stool, seat end against the floor. She could tell he was the more frustrated of the two. He stretched his arms out, shook them, then rested his hands against his hips. The shorter fellow spoke softly about the matter, but Darla was unable to make out what he was saying as she turned her head around to view the opposite end of the hallway. At the far end, a blue door with a black handle was in view.

Shaking her head in confusion, she kept running through all the possible scenarios as to what had happened, how she had gotten here, and where this place even was. Nothing added up.

Darla touched her forehead. What was she going to do? She thought about stepping back and closing the door for posterity. That way, nothing and nobody would ever get to her. But it also meant that she would never escape. She thought of her two young, beautiful children.

With a sudden jolt of courage, Darla stepped out of the bedroom, praying that she wouldn't get caught. As she entered the hallway, Darla stood facing the two men as she crept back to the blue door. Her gaze was fixated on the men in the living room. She saw the taller man pick up the stool again and raise it above his shoulders just as she reached the blue door. With her eyes still focused down the hallway, she moved her hands behind her as she felt for the black handle. Grasping it and twisting, she felt the door slowly open. As the tall stranger swung and hit the window again, Darla opened the door and snuck inside, pushing the door shut behind herself.

Once inside, she found she was in a bathroom, bright light streaming in from a skylight above her. Stepping to the middle and looking up, Darla saw blue sky and the tips of tall pine trees dancing and swaying in the wind. As she looked around, she saw no light switch. There were no cupboards and only a few towels stacked on a shelf beside the bathtub. Everything, except the towels, was blue.

The room—this whole place— nothing made sense.

Pausing her search, Darla looked down and found she was wearing a gray cardigan sweater with a white T-shirt underneath, dark blue jeans, and white socks. Sticking her hands into her pockets and swishing her fingers around, she pulled out a photograph. Holding it under the skylight, she saw the smiles of Luke and Olivia with their arms around each other. Her late husband, Evan, was behind them—all with gleaming smiles. It was her favourite photograph of them, on a trip to visit her relatives in Haiti. Seeing this picture, Darla hoped that maybe this would trigger a memory of how she'd arrived, but nothing came to her. One thing she did know though was that was by far the strangest thing to happen to her in all her thirty-three years.

Darla decided she had no choice left but to confront the two men. She took slow and tentative steps to the other end of the hallway, where both men still had their backs turned to her. The taller man lifted the stool upwards, taking another few strides forward before once again driving the stool against the window. This would be the last time he would do so as the stool blew apart on impact. Two legs flew to the floor as the other two stayed tightly gripped in his hands, the seat landing and spinning like a plate by his feet until it lost all momentum. Neither spoke. The shorter fellow stayed still with his arms crossed, and the taller man tossed the remaining legs against the wall in frustration. Darla then took her final step and the floor creaked.

2

She froze, and both men turned. There, Darla stood, pressing her back against the wall. Both men stared at her, though they didn't say anything at first. She stood still, stiff with fear. Her eyes slowly roamed the eerie, bare space she found herself in, seeing a living room with a large gray clock on the wall as she looked for potential routes of escape. To her right, there was a kitchen with an island counter in the centre and a couple more of the black wooden stools around it. To her left, a four-step staircase led down to the middle-section of the house. It was there she saw a red door. The men must have been able to tell that she was both terrified and confused.

Though there was only silence, body language proved to be the louder than anything in the room. The taller fellow cleared his throat, causing Darla to catch his glare. He stood broad-shouldered and looked to be in his early sixties, weighing a good two-twenty, and his long white hair was parted around a weathered face. He looked to be the type of man that had many stories to tell.

"Hello," he said, but only silence followed.

Darla didn't have her breathing under control. Her heart was pumping at a rapid pace, and a cold sweat was brewing. The shorter man took a step forward, giving her an almost robotic smile. He was square shaped wearing a green sweater and blue jeans, and he looked to be in his late thirties, give or take, with thick dark eyebrows that nobody could miss. He gave her an awkward wave. "Hello, I'm Jesse," he said.

Darla stared at him, terrified, seemingly unable to speak.

"And I'm Ken," the taller man added.

"Wh-why do you have me here?" Darla asked, finally building up the courage to speak.

"Have... you... here? You've got the wrong idea, Miss. We didn't kidnap you or anything," Ken said, giving her a strange glare as he combed his white hair back with his fingers.

Jesse took one step forward, and when he did, Darla took a step back. He stopped, raising his left hand calmly. "Ken and I just met. We've both woken up without a clue of how we got here. Would that be the case with you too…umm…"

"Darla," she answered with regret. "My name is Darla."

"Why the hell did you give him your name? Why?" she thought.

Ken shot in, "Darla. Well, it's a good time to ask. Would you have any idea how—"

"No," she said, shaking her head.

"Okay, Darla. Jesse and I aren't going to hurt you."

Darla snapped her eyes back and forth between them. "You two usually have women wake up all alone in a strange house, just coming to say hello?"

Ken shook his head. "Darla, we didn't put you here."

"How do I know that?" she replied.

"You just... You'll have to trust us, I guess," Ken said, shrugging his shoulders.

"Trust takes longer to build than thirty seconds, mister," Darla said tensely. Should she be that assertive with these strangers? What if they had latent, violent tendencies? Would she ever make it out alive?

There was a pause. Ken and Jesse stared at one another before Jesse spoke. "Darla, Ken and I can't seem to get out of this house."

She tilted her head. None of this made any sense. She was so exhausted, so tired. Being suspicious and having her guard up felt like a huge burden. It would be much easier to just go along with their narrative, even if it meant she could end up dead. "What do you mean?"

Jesse continued, "We tried to open the door, but it seems to be locked. The knob won't twist, and the lock above won't slide. And the windows…well, they just won't open. As you undoubtedly saw, we've even tried breaking them—"

Ken interrupted, looking over at Jesse with a frown. "*I* tried breaking them; it was useless. Bulletproof glass, I reckon. Check out the door, though. See for yourself," he finished. Jesse nodded, and turning to Darla, he gave a slow grin.

Darla slid her back towards the door, turning and going down the steps to the main entrance. The door was bright red with a black doorknob, and a vertical window sat to the right, from ceiling to floor, at shoulder to shoulder-width. Darla noticed a brown wooden porch just outside.

Grabbing hold of the handle, Darla jiggled the doorknob, which posed restraint. As she attempted to open the door, she kept checking back over her shoulder. The unease of the two men lingered, tickling her spine. Back at it and pinching the slide lock that was above the doorknob, Darla twisted with every muscle to turn it north, but her attempts were fruitless.

"We told you!" Ken shouted from the living room.

Darla balled her fist as she leaned against the locked door. Tears of frustration were now begging to be released. Taking in a breath, Darla shut her eyes and rolled her head over her shoulders. She ran her fingers along the seam of the door, then one of the windows. Shifting, Darla stood in front of the window. Leaning back, she gave it the best kick she could, but she only succeeded in falling to the floor. Eyes glaring at the ceiling, tears came trickling down her cheeks that Darla couldn't hold in. "This is a nightmare," she muttered.

To her right, Darla noticed stairs that she assumed led to a basement of sorts. Light from there caught her attention. Getting up, she wiped her tears and went over to investigate. Carefully, she descended the steps, not wanting Ken or Jesse to hear her. Once downstairs, Darla found that the basement had three sofas and a light hanging right in the middle—similar to the one in the kitchen. There were no windows on the blue walls. Suddenly, creaks in the floorboards above caught her attention. Darla listened, following the noise. The steps came from the hallway, and the voice that spoke was, again, one she did not recognize.

3

As she came up the stairs, Darla immediately noticed the new stranger. Standing tall, he was bald and broad-shouldered with a heavy beard. Wearing only a black sweater and jeans, he appeared to be in his fifties. The man stood with his guard up, distrust and stress evident in his eyes. His glare struck Darla. As she stood at the mid-section of the house, the man's shoulders turned to her, and he asked, "Do you have any clue what's goin' on here?" Darla only shook her head, stepping to the upper level and keeping her eyes on the stranger as she did so. Her first instinct was to shield herself, to not be seen.

"What's your name?" he asked.

She hesitated. Who were these men? What kind of a sick abduction was this?

"What is your name, miss, please."

"Darla," she said, softly.

He took a step forward—one of ease. His gaze started at her feet and crawled up slowly to meet her eyes. Once there, he smiled. "Name's Robert. How'd a beautiful young lady like you get here?"

Darla shivered when he spoke. "I don't know. I can't remember how," she admitted.

"Looks like that's all of us then, huh," Robert replied loudly, still keeping his eyes on Darla. After checking her out once more—this time from top to bottom—he turned back to Ken and Jesse. "So, you've tried opening all the doors and windows? I assume all that fuckin' banging I heard was you two trying to break them?"

Ken gave Robert a nod. "That's correct." He then made his way to the first sofa and took a seat. Jesse then followed and joined him.

Robert frowned as he watched the two. "Is this really the time to get comfy?" he asked.

Ken shrugged. "I've been swingin' all morning, friend. I just need to sit down to process all this."

"You need time to process? How long have you been up? Have you tried the doors? Givin' it a real go I mean. Using strength. Or did you just twist the knob like an old pussy?"

Jesse chuckled.

"Don't fuckin' laugh!" Robert barked.

"You haven't tried the skylight in the bathroom, have you?" Darla chipped in.

"Skylight?" Ken said in surprise.

15

"Oh, well, whadda you know. Another way to escape. Look at you three; this bullshit ends now. Why did I wake up here, huh? Some sort of game you like to play with the wealthy? Is it money you want?" Robert spat at them.

Darla stared, speechless.

"Tell me what's going on!" Robert said with force.

There was a lengthy pause and then Ken stood up, his face twitching in irritation. Darla saw Ken clenching his fist while rapping his knuckles against his leg. "You think we're lying to you? How do we know you're not doing this to us?"

Robert stepped closer. "Wanna play a fuckin' game? Come on!" He enticed Ken, beckoning him forward. "Let's go, tough guy. Let's play! Come on, come on!"

"Enough, please!" Darla shouted. She couldn't take the noise anymore.

"Shut up," Robert replied, not even bothering to look at her as he spoke.

"No. Enough. This is bullshit. You're not the only one who wants out," Darla said, terrified by the behaviour.

Ken didn't say a word. He stood still, taking a moment to shut his eyes and inhale. Slowly, he stopped rapping his knuckles against his leg. Opening his eyes, he smiled at Robert, muttered, "Not worth it," and then sat back down.

After he did so, Robert relaxed, yet he seemed disappointed he couldn't take a swing at him. "Come on, Kenny-boy, you gonna listen to some chick?" he tried.

"Fuck you," Darla said anxiously before Ken could respond, in no mood to put up with Robert's shit.

He turned and smiled. "Nah, bitch, fuck you."

"You want to be a prick, fine, go ahead, check the door, the windows, everything," Darla said. She then leaned against the wall, arms crossed and staring at Robert. He nodded, smiled, then walked past her, storming towards the door. Darla watched as he got there, stopped, and looked through the window. Grabbing onto the doorknob, Robert twisted it hard. He then huffed and puffed as he tried to undo the lock.

"Come on," he said under his breath. He stood for a few moments, deciding what to do next. He eventually settled on pulling the door. "COME ON!" he let out as he let go. Darla turned and saw Ken and Jesse, sitting, listening, and shaking their heads.

"The best option I think, right now, is to wait for the owners to stop by. This is clearly some mistake," Jesse said.

Ken shook his head. "I don't think so. Honestly, what rational person locks people up in a house? One that has no way out too," he added.

"I'm just saying," Jesse said, looking down at his feet as they heard Robert coming back up the stairs.

"Oh, for Christ's sake!" he cried out in frustration. He headed over to the windows, checking for a handle, but he quickly realised there was nothing. Slamming his hand against the window, Robert couldn't help but let out a chuckle. "Can't be real. This can't be fucking real." Turning to them all, he added, "How are you all not freaked out by this shit?"

Ken shot up, unable to contain his bottled-up wrath. Bolting forward, Ken clung onto Robert's shirt underneath his black jacket with a tight fist just below his neck. It happened within seconds, and none were prepared. Ken held him tight—flush red in the face and neck—and screamed, "This isn't a fucking dream! We didn't put you here, asshole! Can't you fucking listen?"

Jesse stayed put, watching with his legs crossed and fingers laced together as the drama erupted. Darla stepped back as the violence unfolded.

Robert struggled as he pushed Ken away, trying to get his hands off him as Ken shoved him up against the window. "What the fuck, man!" Robert said to him.

Ken, with fire in his eyes, continued his rage. "Why would we want to be stuck anywhere with *you*?"

Robert forced his hand toward Ken's face and shoved him away. Taking a few steps back, Ken stopped, brushed his white hair back, and stood in front of Robert, taking deep breaths of rage. Darla moved away as the sight of the man led her to think he might explode. Ken's eyes began to flutter, and his breathing started to slow its pace. Robert stepped back, fixing his jacket. Ken didn't say a word; he closed his mouth and began to breathe with a meditative technique. His knuckles rapped on his leg again as he tried to calm himself. The room was tense as they all watched Ken do his thing.

"Psycho," Robert muttered as he turned to walk away, but as he did so, he came to an abrupt stop. Darla noticed him staring down the hallway. As she turned, she saw what Robert was looking at—a young late-twenty-something-year-old man with a blond buzz-cut, in a black tux with the bow tie undone, stood leaning against the wall at the end of the hallway. He was hungover by the looks of it.

Rubbing his face and shaking his head at the scene he had just witnessed, the young stranger gave a laugh. "Damn, I thought the party was over last night."

4

"Who are you?" Robert asked, but the guy just slugged off the wall, dragging his feet to the kitchen. "Hey, man, I'm talking to you," Robert tried again, yet the guy just went straight to the sink.

Opening cupboards, he seemed to be looking for something. He opened them all but found each one empty. "Folks, where're those glasses? Phillip's got himself a hangover," he said, loud and clear for the others to hear.

"Your name's Phillip?" Darla asked.

The young man turned around, aiming his fingers like guns towards her. "Pow-pow, bingo-bingo." He then spun back around to the sink.

"You think you're a comedian?" Robert asked, losing his patience immediately with the little shit, and Jesse let out a laugh. Robert turned to him, and Jesse stopped and nodded apologetically.

Phillip turned the tap of the sink, but nothing came out. He frowned as he waited, twisting it again, but still, no water appeared. Waving his hand underneath, even leaning in, Phillip listened for anything that might suggest water was on its way. Eventually, he turned around and looked at the others. "What's with the sink?" he asked.

Darla spoke up. "Do you know what's going on here?"

Phillip only glared at her. "I'm going to the fridge." He then nodded and stepped away from the sink.

As Phillip opened the fridge, he turned and looked back. "Strange way to store the food," he said.

By now, Ken was relaxing somewhat. Once he had returned to reality, he seemingly noticed Phillip for the first time. "Who the hell is this?" he asked.

Robert was keeping his eye on Phillip, but he was also weirded out by what the young man had discovered. "Phillip," Robert said softly, answering Ken while still fixated on the discovery.

All the food had been put in yellow plastic zip bags, all lined neatly side by side. "Fuck, you all really love yellow," Phillip said as he reached in for a bag.

"Wait," Darla said, and they all turned to her. "Don't eat it," she begged.

Phillip looked at her. "Umm, and you are?" he asked.

Darla stepped up and slammed the fridge door. "You're not eating this," she said, and Phillip looked at her in disgust.

"Hey, bitch, nobody tells me what to do."

"The food could be poisoned for all we know," she explained.

Phillip paused, trying to understand. "All of this has gone bad?"

"No," she said. "None of us know what's going on right now. The food may not be good for us."

"*Or* it'll be the only food we'll have for some time," Ken added as he sat himself down again.

Phillip pivoted and let out a laugh. "Was this not—" He stopped, staring around the room, the fog slowly clearing in his mind. "This is not where I partied last night, is it?" he asked.

Darla shook her head. "I highly doubt it."

"So, you've also never been here before or have any memory of how you got here?" Robert asked.

Phillip thought for a moment, shook his head, and said, "No." Panic then seemed to set in, and he took a step back from them all. "Who are you people?" he asked.

Ken spoke up from the couch. "Buddy, listen—"

"Hey, I'm not your buddy. I'm not anyone's fuckin' buddy. You hear me?" Phillip replied.

Steps down the hallway echoed through the room, interrupting their fighting. The five of them snapped their eyes towards the sound in unison. A man in his thirties with retro-rimmed glasses, wearing a brown blazer and black jeans, stood nervously beside door number 7—the bedroom they assumed he'd just woken in. He was nervous, they could tell. Raising his hand and giving an awkward wave, he said, "I-I'm Floyd. Can someone please tell me what's happening?"

5

"I just can't believe it, sorry," Floyd said. He pushed past Darla and headed to the door.

Phillip followed, "I'm with this guy."

Both made it to the door, but to no one's surprise, they struggled with it. "This isn't funny. Open it," Floyd said.

Darla shrugged. "We are not playin' you guys."

Ken got up from his seat, walked over to the kitchen, and had a look at the taps. He turned them on, yet nothing worked. Opening the kitchen cabinet doors underneath, Ken went to check the plumbing, but there were no pipes, no nothing. It was nothing more than a mock set up.

"Open the goddamn door!" Phillip demanded.

"We can't," Robert explained, and the others nodded in agreement.

Floyd stood in front of the window, staring at the woods. Stepping closer and gazing all around, the trees seemed to wrap around the house. Running upstairs, he looked out of the windows. Darla watched as Floyd began to panic. Backtracking from the window, he headed back into the hallway. He stopped once he saw Darla, pressing his glasses up against the bridge of his nose.

"Please, this isn't a game you're playing, is it? Just be honest with me. People have played games with me my whole life. It's not funny. Just tell me the truth," he implored, begging for a proper answer.

Darla shook her head, almost feeling ashamed. "I-I just woke up, Floyd. Just like you." Floyd nodded, then continued down the hallway to his room, attempting to open the window there instead.

Ken stepped into the bathroom, checking the sink. Again, no water flowed when the taps were turned on. These two squeaked and required grease. Ken tried the tub as well. Nothing. His last option was the toilet. Opening the lid, he found there was no water in the bowl. He even checked the toilet tank, lifting off the heavy porcelain lid, yet no water was inside, not even any mechanics. It was plain empty. Ken caught himself in the mirror on the way out and muttered, "This place fake?"

Phillip paced around the living room with the others, thrashing his arms back and forth as if he was trying to get his blood flowing. "I just. This isn't fucking real, right? I'm in a nightmare." The others stood and sat around him, watching.

Darla almost answered until Ken spouted, "I doubt it's a nightmare. Feels pretty real to me... buddy."

Once Ken said this, Phillip stopped pacing and shot his eyes towards him. "What the fuck did I tell you?"

"We need to calm down," Darla interrupted.

Phillip pointed towards Ken. "I'm not your buddy, alright? In this place, right here, I'm no one's friend."

"That may be a poor choice of words," Jesse said as he sat comfortably.

"Fuck you," Phillip said. "Fuck all of you. Outside this house, I would never associate with you peasants."

The whole room tensed as Phillip's words were received with disgust.

"Peasants? Is that right...*buddy*?" Ken said to Phillip.

Phillip approached Ken as Darla tried to get in the way again.

"Yeah, that's right!" Phillip said. "I fucking said it. Peasants. People like you have been serving me my whole life. You're all pond scum."

"Enough!" Darla shouted at Phillip, but he wilfully ignored her.

"Fuckin' pond scum!" he raged. "Make yourself useful, Kenny-Boy, and get me some water."

"Go. To. Hell," Ken replied, doing all he could to restrain his rage.

Floyd walked up to try and interject.

"Forget about this asshole and have a seat, Ken," Floyd said.

"I don't listen to you. And, Phillip, you haven't a clue what's coming if you keep with this attitude. Keep spilling those—"

"You're fucking pond scum!" Phillip shouted again as he leaned towards Ken, just pushing past Darla.

Ken snapped and lunged forward, hooking his hand around the back of Phillip's head. He pulled Phillip towards himself, causing the younger man to lose his balance. Before he landed on his knees, Ken swung his right fist, which collided with Phillip's left cheek. He took the hit, then fell to his knees. Darla went to grab Phillip as Robert and Floyd charged for Ken. He was able to get two more swings in before Robert and Floyd checked him against the fridge doors, pressing him tightly against his back. Darla tugged on Phillip's shirt collar, bringing him back to a sitting position.

"Fuck you, rich boy!" Ken cried out.

"Fuck you, peasant!" Phillip cried back over Floyd's shoulder.

Darla stuck herself between the two, getting in the way as Ken attempted to go at Phillip again. It was up to her to break up the fight. She stood in front, raising her hands, looking him in the eye. "Enough. Enough of this," she said, yet Ken still tried to get her out of the way.

"This fucker isn't going to get away with calling us that!" Ken shouted, pointing with furious rage towards Phillip. Robert and Floyd kept Ken pinned to the fridge as he struggled to get at Phillip.

"Come on, you fuck. Letting the lady get in your way?" Phillip said with an arrogant smile, flushed red in his face. Ken took a breath, his upper lip curling as he struggled to maintain himself.

"Don't let him get to you," Darla begged Ken.

"Little fucking late for that," Ken admitted. He backed off into the living room, shaking off his fury. Ken sat beside Jesse, who was again sitting comfortably, fingers laced and watching the show.

Robert and Floyd pushed Phillip back, but he spat at their feet, fixing his tux and barking, "Fuckin' assholes!"

Robert took a step forward, then Phillip, cowardly, took a step back. Robert raised his finger at him about to speak, but Phillip shot his words in before he could. "What the fuck you gonna do? Huh, What the fuck you gonna do, bro?" he challenged, smiling, arms out and eyes wide.

Robert shook his head. "Millennials," he retorted and joined the others.

"Okay, I can't deal with any more of this," Darla said. She dug into her pockets and swished her hands around. The others stared at her while she did this, all in wonder. Finally, Darla pulled out what looked like a small, 4-by-6 photograph. Flipping it around, she held the photo before her, making sure they all got a good look. "This here is a photo of my late husband and my two babies, Luke and Olivia, 8 and 11. Right now, they're terrified because their mother isn't with them. If I'm not there, that means they're alone. Every second that ticks by makes me feel just a little sicker knowing that they're scared that I'm not around. I. Will. Get. Home. So… the quicker we all start acting like adults, the better.

"All of us are scared as hell and even more confused. But, by God, you think we're going to get home acting like morons? Tell me one thing we've done so far—anything— that has gained us any progress? You know this house is defective. So much about it isn't right. None of us have any memory of how we got here. It's *Twilight Zone* shit, I know, but hell, can we all pull it together to figure out a solution to this problem instead of just adding to it?"

Everyone in the room paused their squabbling.

"You're right," Floyd said, smiling at Darla.

"I know." Darla put the photo back into her pocket. "We've got food, but it's really limited. We've—"

"I say we wait," Jesse interrupted.

"Wait?" asked Ken.

"Yeah, like I said before, somebody owns this house. Why not just wait til they get back?" Jesse scanned the room, searching for an agreeable face.

"And then what? Shake their dicks and say hello?" Robert said.

"No more waiting," Darla said. "We figure out a way out of here."

Floyd raised his hand. "May I just say something... There are six of us here, but there are seven rooms. Who's the last guest?"

PHILLIP

Fixing his tie, Phillip kept eye contact with himself in the mirror. Adjusting his jacket and rolling his neck around, he jumped up and down in one spot. He was pumping himself up and getting that blood flow going. "You give it to him," he said, smacking his fist against his chest. Phillip leaned in closer to the mirror and fixed his hair, doing so for 10 minutes. After he made his way through his mansion— the one that Daddy paid for—he went down the spiral staircase and out the large, mahogany wooden doors.

Stepping through, the maid said, "Have a wonderful day, Phillip," but he didn't answer, he just kept on out the door.

The chauffeur was already out of the car, dressed in a fine white suit, with the door open for Phillip to get in.

"Beautiful day today, sir," the chauffeur said.

As Phillip was about to step into the car, he stopped and took a gander at the sunny sky. "Same fuckin' shit every day, Rob."

Rob, the chauffeur, nodded, put on a happy face, and shut the door gently behind him. After climbing into the driver's seat, Rob looked in the rear-view mirror and asked, "Your father's office, sir?"

Phillip brought his gaze to the driver and gave him a nod.

The black car, with its beautiful shine glaring under the sun, went into the busy street, traveled across the city, then parked out front of the office. Phillip got out of the car and leaned in, saying, "Look, Rob, I don't know how long this is going to take. I'm going to talk to this son of a bitch. I don't know how long but sit tight."

Rob nodded and gave a smile. "I will do that, si—" he started, but Phillip slammed the door and left before he could finish.

Phillip looked up as he approached the front entrance. His father's office building was massive. 'BNC Studios, Toronto.' The lobby was busy with people coming in and out, and every chair held hopefuls of all courts in the entertainment business. Phillip went to the main desk and stood there while the head receptionist, Rebecca—who Phillip knew and had even tried to sleep with (she declined)—sat on the phone, smiling at him, raising a finger and signalling to give her a moment. She was busy, but Phillip didn't care.

"I want to speak to my father." Phillip glared at her. Rebecca, the phone still to her ear, raised her hand again to ask for just a moment.

Phillip slammed his fist against the counter, loudly enough for the others working to take notice. They sat awkwardly as they watched their co-worker deal with the spoilt child. Rebecca's face went blank as she stared at the son of her boss, demanding she switch her time over to him.

She gave Phillip a nod, then, speaking into the phone, she said, "I'm sorry, may I get back to you very short—"

"I want to speak to my father!" Phillip demanded.

"V-very shortly," Rebecca finished. "Thank you."

She hung up the phone and summoned a smile; Phillip knew it was fake. "How can I help you, Phillip?" she asked, yet Phillip just laughed at the counter, looking at all the staff as they watched him. "I told you I want to speak with my father. Give me the pass to get to his office."

"I can ring him and let—"

"No, just give me the pass. I want to surprise him."

"Well, Phillip, I can't just do that."

"Why not?"

"Because it's—"

"Rebecca, give me the goddamn pass, NOW! I have very urgent business with him. Business that's extremely important."

"Phillip, I understand, but your father prefers—"

"I don't give a fuck. Give me the pass right now."

"I'm not allowed to, Phillip."

"Rebecca, one day, I'm going to be in charge of this place. My father is getting to an age where he'll be handing me the keys to this castle, not wanting to have the responsibility." Phillip leaned in, gave her a smile, and looked her in the eye. "If you don't give me the pass, I won't forget this moment, and when I become king of this castle, I will not think twice about letting go of a receptionist or two. What do you say, Rebecca? Should I look into getting some replacements?" Phillip glared at her from top to bottom, then he met her eyes and smiled. "Or just one?"

Rebecca, her face blank, clearly stricken by Phillip's comments, muscled up a smile at him. "Of course, Phillip, one moment," she said as she opened a drawer. As she looked, Phillip stared at the others who were working at the large front desk. As his eyes met theirs, all of them turned back and got on with their work. Rebecca raised her hand, pass in her palm, and she reached out toward him across the desk. Phillip snagged it and gave her a wink of pure sleaze as he left.

As he stepped into the elevator, Phillip scanned the pass that allowed him to the very top floor. Once he stepped out, he walked down the hallway leading to his father's office. Phillip passed multiple famous film and television posters of the studio's work. At the end of the hall, Phillip checked himself in the mirror just outside the office, fixing his tie and telling himself, "You got this."

Scanning the pass on a keypad to the right of the door, a light went green, and he opened the door, stepping into another room. His father's secretary, Kate, who Phillip couldn't stand, sat at her desk. Her eyes looked up at his. "Phillip? This is unannounced," she said.

Phillip ignored her and kept walking through. "Is he here?" he asked while he kept his feet moving.

"He is, yes," she replied.

Phillip, going straight for the door, gave her a wink. "Thank you." He opened the door to his daddy's office, slamming it shut right behind him, the echo of the door shaking the walls. There, Phillip's father, John, sat at his desk, not looking up, only lifting his pen that had previously been stroking across the paper.

"What the fuck is your deal?" Phillip asked him.

There was a pause, then John, in his mid-sixties, dressed in his fitted *Burberry* suit, raised his head and placed his pen down. Crossing his arms, he leaned back into his chair.

Kate came in straight after. "I'm sorry, sir, he just—"

But John smiled at her, raising his hand. "It's okay, Kate." Both John and Phillip watched as Kate nodded and left the office, shutting the door behind her.

Phillip walked up to his father, leaned forward, and placed both hands on his desk. "You are a real motherfucker, Dad," Phillip snarled.

"Get your hands off my desk, you child. It's worth more than you," John said, but Phillip shook his head, keeping his hands right where they were.

"You gave the job to Larry? Fucking... Larry?" Phillip said.

John nodded. "That's correct."

"You promised that you'd give that job to me," Phillip said.

John shook his head. "No, I didn't."

"I was next in line for it. I had ideas for the show, and you make him the producer?"

"Phillip, Larry has been a long-time producer for twenty-seven years, why would I offer it to you?"

"You said—"

"No, I didn't say anything. You asked for the job, and I didn't respond. Why would I hire you? A young man with zero experience in production."

"Zero experience?" Phillip let out a laugh, stepping away from the desk. "Zero experience my ass! I've watched you my whole life talk about this shit; you don't think I know my stuff?"

"That's correct."

"But I do."

"No, you don't, and that's why the job goes to Larry."

Phillip paced the room for a moment, his father watching as the boy let off steam. Phillip stopped and turned to his father. "How in the fuck do you think I'll ever run this place if you don't give me a chance to have an entry-level producer position?"

"It's not for anyone—entry level—far from it. And I always hear that talk, Phillip. What makes you think that I'll be leaving you in charge?"

Phillip took a step back. "Who else would take over your position besides me?"

"Anyone who works here. I'd rather have them than you…*boy*."

"I'm next in line!"

John shook his head. "Oh, you man-child, that's not how it works. You don't get to run a multi-billion-dollar corporation just because of your family name. Maybe if you applied yourself and showed some humility in your life— instead of being an egotistical arrogant sob always buying lavish things and spending big money that you never earned on parties and impressing your 'friends'."

"Fuck you. The job is mine."

John shook his head again, adding a little laughter. "Phillip, the other day I tried to get your attention at home, but you couldn't hear me. You were so god damn busy looking at your phone. You've never worked a day in your life, Phillip. You may think you're the man, but you're far from it, and that, I guess, is my fault for not giving you the attention you needed. You've spent more time in front of the mirror than in the workforce. Now, I'm about to say a sentence you've never said in your life. I've got work to do, so, please, be a good little boy and let Daddy get back to it."

Phillip was misty-eyed, clenching his fist, wanting nothing more than to knock the old man's teeth out. He took a breath, watching his dad get back to work, no longer acknowledging him.

"I will have this job!" Phillip cried out.

John, not even lifting his head, hit a button on his office phone. "Hello, Kate, can you escort my little boy out of the building please. He's a nuisance. If he doesn't comply, call security."

John then let go of the button and got back to work. Phillip heard the door open, and Kate stepped in. Phillip spun around to see her, shaking his head. Turning back to his father, Phillip smiled. "You don't know what you're doing, old man."

"I'm deflating your ego, *young* man."

Phillip stormed out of the office and down the elevator. He hardly slowed to throw the pass key towards Rebecca, causing her to duck as it torpedoed toward her. Phillip stepped out of the offices and saw the car idling. Stepping around to the driver's side, Phillip, with great aggression, rapped his knuckles on the window.

As it rolled down, Rob stared at Phillip. "Is everything—"

"Get out of the car, Rob. I need to go for a ride to clear my fuckin' head. Go for a walk by yourself, grab lunch, or do whatever the fuck you want to do."

Phillip dug into his suit jacket pocket and pulled out a money clip.

Rob shook his head. "I'm afraid, sir, I can't—"

"Just do it," Phillip demanded, handing Rob three hundred-dollar bills.

Phillip was soon driving in the busy city—the first time he'd driven in almost two years. "Fuckin' shit head! Motherfucker! Motherfucker!" Phillip yelled. As he drove, he muttered all sorts of things, then he began smacking the steering wheel of the car. "Fuck that piece of shit! Fuck him!"

He drove for an hour, with no idea how he was going to get home. He didn't care where he was, it didn't matter, he just wanted to drive.

Bringing the rear-view mirror down as he was driving, Phillip leaned over, fixing his hair once again. It was short, but he always felt it had to be perfect. As his eyes scanned down, he caught a pimple on the bottom of his lip. Leaning in even farther, eyes back and forth from the road to the mirror, he placed a finger on his lower lip and rolled his eyes.

"Fuck. Come on," he said.

BOOM!

THUMP!

THUMP!

The whole car bounced up and down suddenly, and Phillip hit the brakes. The car squealed on the pavement and let out a scream. Stepping out, Phillip, angry at first, slammed the door shut, ready to take his frustrations out on the world. That was until he turned around. As he did, he let out another scream. A crossing guard dropped her sign and, in her bright orange jacket, ran over to the body lying on the street. Dropping to her knees, she let out a cry to the sky. Phillip's guts sank, and for a moment, he froze in utter shock. Watching the horror unfold, Phillip gathered himself, opened the car door, slipped in, and sped away.

6

The group walked up to door number 6. Still shut, they all crowded near it. Ken was up at the front, and he looked back at the rest of the group. They nodded, so he turned back and said a soft, "Hello?" but there was only silence. Ken tried again. "Hello? Anyone awake in there?" but still, there was no response. Raising his hand, he gave a gentle knock on the door.

"Just open it, man," Robert said over Ken's shoulder.

Ken took a second, nervous as hell, and then he grabbed the knob of the door and twisted it. It gave a click as it opened. Ken pushed the door open slowly; the room seemed to be empty. As Ken was ahead, he was the first inside. He took a half-step into the room.

WHAM!

A fist landed on the right side of his face, and Ken's head whipped to the left. The others, surprised as one, all jumped back. Before Ken could hit the side wall, hands reached out and grabbed him by his denim jacket, pulling him towards the stranger behind door number 6. The large figure of a man spun the half-conscious Ken around and put him in a tight headlock. He was a tall, balding fellow weighing a good three-fifty, wearing a gray hoodie and blue jeans. Darla, Floyd, and Robert moved into the room, and as they did, the large stranger backtracked to the corner, still restraining his hostage.

"Easy," Darla said with her hands out.

"What in the hell is goin' on?" the stranger asked, paranoid, terrified, and tightening his grip around Ken's neck.

"None of us are going to hurt you," Darla pleaded.

"Fuck you! Why do yea' got me?" the stranger cried out. Ken was now flushed red with a bruise already swelling on his face. He was trying to make his begging heard, but he was unable, due to being choked by the man's lumbering arm.

"None of us are going to hurt you. Please, let him go," Floyd begged.

"You gonna cut out my organs or some shit?"

"No! Jesus, man, come on," Robert said in disgust.

"Look, I'm Darla, and this is Floyd. Robert is over here, and well… you've got Ken. The others behind us are Phillip and…"

"Jesse," Jesse finished.

Darla winced at forgetting his name, not too impressed how that moment turned out. "We aren't here to hurt you. Honestly."

"How the fuck do I know you ain't lyin'?" the huge man asked.

"All of us have woken up here, not knowing how or why we are in this house. We didn't do anything to you. Nothing. Let him go, and come outside so we can prove to you that we're telling you the truth," Darla said before digging in her pockets, searching for her picture. The stranger saw this and tightened his grip around Ken's neck.

'Gaah! Plwaassee…cuua……hewlp," Ken gurgled.

She grabbed her photograph and shot her arm out towards the stranger. "Look at them. Those are my children. My name is Darlene, but everybody calls me Darla. I'm a mother of two. I'm a photographer by trade and have run my own business since twenty-eight. I was born in Haiti but moved to Canada when I was six. I had my children in my early twenties." Darla paused as tears began to flow. "I really, really want to be with my children. We all have a life outside these walls. This is all messed up and strange I know, but, my God, we just need you not to hurt him. All of us are scared. All of us are confused. Let him go so we can work on a way to get out of here."

Floyd then spoke up. "I'm Floyd. I'm thirty-three, and I live with my sick mom. Well…she lives with me. I have no kids and no wife or girlfriend, but my mom needs help. That's why I need out of here."

Robert paused and seemed to think 'what the hell'. "I'm Robert, man… nice to meet you," he said, looking at the stranger. "I'm a fifty-one-year-old father to three beautiful kids, with a wonderful wife. I own a chain of car washes… Well, that's it really. I guess.

The stranger began to ease himself off Ken, seeing the desperation on their faces. Jesse rose his hand toward the back. "My name's Jesse. I'm a musician—teacher mainly. Had myself a daughter. She passed. Wife left me. Still, though, I wanna go home."

"I'm Phillip, twenty-four, and I'm an alcoholic."

"And an asshole!" Darla snapped back.

There was a pause, then the stranger let Ken go. Finally, Ken gasped for breath, and Robert held him by his arm and pulled him away from the man.

Darla took a half-step forward. "We're honest. Come out and let us explain everything we know. Please. What's your name?"

The stranger stared at Darla, still hesitant. After a moment, he spoke up again, "Name's Lawrence. I'm a janitor. Fifty-three. Two kids. And real fuckin' confused."

The group gave a feeble laugh.

"This way, follow me," Darla said, guiding him out the room with a smile.

7

Darla stood in the centre of the living room as the others stood around or took a seat. Lawrence strolled out of the hallway, gazing around the place. He squeezed past Darla and walked towards the first living room window, taking a good look at the woods outside.

"So, we all trapped?" Lawrence asked.

Darla nodded behind him. "Yes. It seems so. We need to get going on a way out of here."

Ken came up behind Darla, groaning from the hit he took. Lawrence turned and saw him, feeling no remorse. Ken caught his eye, yet he still sat on the sofa closest to the hallway, keeping a hand on his swollen face.

"Anyone wake up with a phone or any device?" she asked, but nobody answered. Then gradually, everyone shook their heads no.

"Nothing. Just a folded bookmark in my blazer pocket," Floyd said.

"I just have the photograph," Darla said.

The rest of the men sat quietly until Phillip spoke. "Well, great. We all woke up with nothing of good use. So, what's the plan to get out of this shithole?" he asked, and everyone just seemed to eye each other.

"We find a way out. First, we all attempt the door together. If that doesn't work, Lawrence and I can go at the skylight in the bathroom, see if it can be opened or try and break the thing. Lawrence are you comfortable having me on your shoulders?" she asked.

Lawrence turned to her. "I should be askin' you that."

"Well, I am," Darla said. "You four can search for any openings. Maybe even kick a cavity in the wall? Possibly dig our way through," she said, turning towards Jesse, Ken, Floyd, and Phillip.

Floyd smiled. "Break our way out? I like it. Give the owners of this place something to fix."

"That's right." Darla then turned to Robert. "You search what's in the kitchen. If there's anything we could use. Also, inventory what's in the fridge for us."

"Fuck you," Robert said.

Darla should have been surprised by his words, but she wasn't. "Excuse me?"

"I'm not taking orders from anyone," Robert said.

"And why not?" asked Floyd.

"You have a problem with me?" Darla asked.

Robert looked at the room, then back at her, crossing his arms and giving her a huff of disapproval. "You think I'm going to take orders from some thirty-something? Think again, 'cause it ain't going to happen."

Darla smirked. "Is that right?"

Robert nodded. "That's right." Then he finished with a kissing motion with his lips towards her.

Darla scoffed in disgust.

"I like where this is going," Phillip snarled.

"Don't be a prick," Floyd said to Robert.

"Shut it," Robert said.

Darla turned to the rest of the guys. "Does anyone have a problem with what I've just mentioned?"

No one spoke, only the nods of their heads approving the orders given.

"Good." She smiled. "Let's get at it. As for you, Robert, do what you want. Everyone else, let's tackle that door."

Ken raised his left hand, with his other covering his bruised and swollen face. "I'm going to lie down."

8

First, he took a deep breath, then Lawrence went bolting towards the red door, slamming himself against it. His shoulder went sore in an instant. The big man took a step back, shook off the pain, and did it again. But the door stayed shut. Lawrence stepped back once more, shaking off the sharp sting in his shoulder. His eyes caught the group, and he rolled his shoulder, but nothing was said. He did it one last time, but it ended with the same result. Floyd attempted as well, once Lawrence stepped away, just for the sake of it. But his skinny frame made it almost laughable to watch. It was time for Plan B.

Lawrence pulled his sleeves up and grabbed the knob on the red door. Behind him was Phillip, and as he tried to wrap his hands around Lawrence, he couldn't quite reach.

"Havin' a tough time, sport?" Lawrence asked Phillip.

"Yes, you're a fat fuck."

His eyes snapped at Phillip, not in the mood for his bullshit, but Phillip gave a smile and a wink. All Phillip could do was grip onto those soft, love handles of his. Floyd then grasped Phillip, Darla held around Floyd, and then Jesse was in the back. Robert stayed watching from above as the train readied themselves to pull.

"On three!" Darla shouted.

1, 2, **3**!

The group pulled as hard as they could with all their strength. Their feet were sliding on the floor, unable to get proper traction. Jesse, behind them, was the first to slip and fall, landing on his ass. They stopped for a moment to allow him to get up—all of them panting for breath. Robert stood above in the living room, laughing at the crew's attempts. Darla saw Robert do this, and it lit another fire inside her.

"Again!" she ordered.

The guys shook it off, hooking around one another again.

Lawrence could feel the palms of his hands already feeling worn. "We got this! Pull harder now!" Lawrence gripped, and the crew made the train. Their feet were planted to the ground, doing what they could to get the best grip.

"On three again!" Floyd ordered this time.

1, 2, **3**!

The crew pulled again but for no result. Lawrence ended up letting go, causing the line to drop. All of them lay on their backs, with Robert's laugh raining on them from above.

Darla sat up and saw the men catching their breath. "Okay. It's okay," she told them. She was the first to spring up, fixing herself, and she called them to order. "Let's get at it, guys. Lawrence, you're with me. The rest of you get to your jobs."

Lawrence and Darla walked into the bathroom. She held one of the stools from the kitchen in her hands, and both looked at the skylight, trying to see a handle, but there was nothing. Darla nudged Lawrence's shoulder. The space in the bathroom was tight with both in there. Darla still couldn't believe how big this man was.

"You got me?" Darla asked, and Lawrence nodded. Grabbing the stool, Darla stepped onto the toilet, then onto the bathroom sink, giving her the height to hook her legs onto Lawrence's shoulders. Lifted up, Darla was as close as she could be to the skylight. Lawrence handed her the stool. Keeping his head low, he allowed her the room to wind up a swing, and so Darla gave it a go, slamming the stool into the window.

Floyd and Phillip walked around each wall of the house, checking everywhere for a possible opening, anything that could be a starting point for a way out. Jesse watched the guys do all the work as they searched for an opening of any kind, and then he slowly migrated to the couch. Floyd caught this but kept going. "God damn lazy," he muttered.

Robert eventually gave in to Darla's order. Pulling the food out of the fridge and placing it on the island counter, he scanned the yellow bags. There was:

- 4 loaves of bread
- 8 bags of sliced meats
- 12 bunches of lettuce

With the amount of food, give or take, Robert thought they'd have to ration so they could at least last a week and a half—if they were careful. Robert then noticed the block of kitchen knives right beside the refrigerator. He tried to pull it forward, but the wooden block resisted. He couldn't move it. Checking the bottom, Robert saw that it seemed as though it had been glued to the counter. Wrapping his arms around the block, he pulled, yet it didn't move an inch.

"Okay," Robert said to himself. Counting each knife, he saw there were seven. The block might be stuck, but the knives were able to come out, and they were genuine.

Meanwhile, Darla swung for the last time, and the stool thudded as it hit. Nothing happened. The skylight was as indestructible as all the other windows. Her arms were now tired—as was Lawrence, still carrying Darla on his shoulders. Wrestling her frustration, Darla, within seconds, lost the fight, and tears began flowing down her cheeks. Lawrence began to lower himself, not saying a word, and Darla took the hint, swinging a leg, getting on top of the bathroom counter, and stepping off onto the floor.

"Have we checked all the bedroom windows?" Lawrence asked.

Darla had her chin high, slightly looking away from Lawrence and trying her best not to show her tears. Wiping her cheeks, she shook her head no. Lawrence rested his palm on her shoulder. "Well, let's go have a look and see what we can do."

Jesse watched as Floyd held his hand against the wall at the front of the house, gently knocking to find any cavity. Listening in, wrapping his knuckles gently, Floyd stopped.

"Find something?" Jesse asked, but Floyd didn't answer. Jesse smiled. "You're all wasting your time."

Phillip, who stood behind Floyd, glanced over at Jesse and gave him the bird, and Jesse shook his head and shut his eyes. Floyd stopped knocking and stood back, then with a hefty step forward, he drove his foot into the wall, disappearing into the blue.

Lawrence and Darla had begun to try and break the small window in Room 7 when they heard the bang. They stepped out and saw Floyd kicking into the blue wall viciously. Phillip immediately began to get excited, dropping to his knees and tearing at the wall, tossing the bits behind him in a desperate attempt to escape. Floyd then stopped kicking and did the same. That was until he hit what felt like a solid block. It was dark in the hole, but the more they tore away, the clearer they all could see. Behind all the plaster and drywall was something more robust. Floyd and Phillip turned to one another, then to the rest of the crew who were behind them.

Darla had a look over Floyd's shoulder, "Is that—"

"Cement."

While he stuck his hands in the front pocket of his green sweater, Jesse gave a laugh. "Waste of time, my friends."

9

"We have enough food for a week and a half, give or take," Robert said, "And, of course, no water."

The others stood around the island counter in the kitchen, with Jesse still on the couch. The room slumped to an even greater depression. Stress began to build again as the words escaped Robert's mouth.

"Fuck," Phillip said. "How fucking long can you live without water?"

"Three days I believe, but for you with that hangover, I'd say less," Ken said as he walked out of the hallway and into the living room.

Phillip pushed away from the table. "Oh, fucking great. Thank you. Feeling real tip-top now, you son of a bitch."

Ken shrugged, still holding his swollen face. "I'm just being honest."

"Honest, right. Fuck you and your honesty, Ken." He held his hips and began to breathe deeply in what seemed like the start of a panic attack before he began to cry. No comfort came from the group. There was only silence as Phillip sobbed.

"How's that fridge being powered?" Darla asked, and she pointed to the kitchen light. "And that light? Anyone else notice how there are no switches in this place?"

"I noticed that," Floyd answered.

"Me too," Ken admitted.

"Should we move the fridge? See where the wires lead to?" Jesse suggested.

"You going to help or watch?" Floyd asked.

"Hey now," Jesse said.

"Let's do it, but I doubt we'll have any luck," Robert said.

Lawrence approached the fridge. Grasping it as Robert did too, both tugged the refrigerator with every ounce of strength they had. Nothing moved. Shaking his head in frustration, Robert said, "Feels like it's attached to the fucking floor."

Lawrence let go, slamming his hand against the door. Again, they stood in silence.

"None of us have any options right now, but maybe we should wait. Just a night. Hopefully, we can find some clues. 'Til then, we are going to have to use that food sparingly," Darla said.

Robert rolled his eyes and said with a sneer, "Ah, thanks. You're a real natural leader, Darla dear."

"Enough!" Darla shouted, slamming her fist onto the table. "I won't have this, Robert. I won't."

He smiled, happy that he had lit her fuse. "Yeah, Darla, what? What are you going to do?"

"I won't put up with the sexist bullshit."

He winked at her and smiled. "How am I sexist? Huh? Tell me."

"All I'm trying to do here is figure a way out before we all get cabin fever or die of thirst or hunger. This whole time, so far, everything I've said, you've combated consistently," Darla said.

He chuckled. "Where the fuck do you get off?"

"Goddamn it, if you want to play leader, then play leader." Darla stepped away from the kitchen and walked back to her bedroom, shutting the door. She needed some peace. As she lay on her bed, a fountain of tears flowed down her face. Covering her mouth to try and soften the sound of her sobs, Darla lay on her right side so she could still face the door. Pulling out the photograph of her children, she held it tightly in her hand against her chest.

The vision of her father as he lay on the sidewalk powdered in snow, drenched in his blood, flooded her mind. Darla shook her head, trying to erase the image. But, like a nasty disease, it wouldn't go away so easily. Her heart rate sped up as the memory played like a film. It was like she was there again. She was terrified, stepping closer to the scene.

The blood was pouring from his stomach, his hand reaching out to grab her own. His eyes, rolling back into his skull, with his lips mumbling words she couldn't make out.

10

Night came, and Darla had stayed in her room since the altercation. Lying on her back, she stared at the ceiling, thinking of her children. She was doing all she could to piece this together, but nothing fit. Tears trickled down her cheeks as she found herself overrun with fear and frustration. Covering her mouth, she tried to silence her cry, not wanting any of the men to hear. Darla overheard someone leave their bedroom; she didn't bother to get up and check.

Ken dragged his feet to the living room. His head felt as though it was full of water. Every sound seemed to irritate him, and that curse of a light in the kitchen—with its warm glow sizzling his eyes. Ken knew he had a concussion; he was sure of it. Sitting himself down, he rested his head back against the couch, trying to ignore the pain and his ravishing need for a drink. The rest of the group were in their rooms or downstairs–he could hear them. The living room was silent, but the ticking of the large clock beside him jabbed at his attention.

TICK. TICK. TICK. TICK.

Ken wanted it to stop. Getting up from the couch, he moved over and stood in front of the large clock—one minute to 9:00 pm. Looking closer, Ken watched the clock tick. It was covered by a glass he knew couldn't break. "Fucking STOP!" Ken shouted, but that clock kept going with every tick now feeling like a pin pricking his brain.

TICK. TICK. TICK. TICK. TICK. TICK. TICK. TICK.

Ken stepped away, and that was when he saw it. Someone was outside, standing by the trees in the woods. Ken moved closer to the window, trying to make them out.

Walking over to the other window, he gave himself a better view on who was outside. Whoever it was, both she and Ken were now staring at one another. The woman, standing still, was only wearing what looked to be a nightgown. It didn't seem right, but she was too far away to see clearly. He waved to her, and she, staying put, tilted her head and raised her hand almost in a soulless way as if the poor woman had never been waved to before.

The return of the gesture didn't feel right. Something was up, and Ken could feel it. As he looked closer, he saw that the woman's nightgown wasn't plain white; it had something on it. Focusing as best he could with his good eye,

Ken saw what it was. Her gown was peppered with blood. His focus readjusted as his eyes gazed up to hers; the woman smiled a smile that was not natural. One that shot a shiver down his spine and spun a knot in his stomach. Ken took a step back, covering his mouth. "Jesus Christ, Jesus Christ," he muttered from underneath the palm of his hand.

TICK. TICK. TICK.

The clock then struck 9:00 pm, and the lock on the big red door suddenly slid open.

ACT II

LAWRENCE

He wolfed it all down—his whole dinner. In disgust, everyone at the table couldn't help but watch. Lawrence chewed and drank, chewed and drank, until there was nothing left besides whatever fell on his shirt and lap. The others at the table, his neighbours and wife, sat uncomfortably as he slopped his food up. The dinner was silent, difficult to get back on track from the show Lawrence, unexpectedly, put on. After the hour passed and the friends said goodbye, Lawrence helped his wife, Susan, with the dishes.

They scrubbed away, standing in silence as they cleaned. Lawrence couldn't help but notice Susan was quiet and seemed somewhat distant.

"What's wrong?" he asked as he scrubbed a plate. Susan glared at him, then brought her chin down to her chest, staring at the plate she was drying. He could tell she was muscling up a sentence to say. Taking a breath, she said, "Look, I'm worried again."

"About what?" Lawrence asked, placing the plate back in the sink, then his hands on the counter.

"Your health," she said with concern.

"My health? My health is A-Okay."

"Lawrence, I don't think it is."

"But I feel great, hun."

"That doesn't matter. It doesn't mean you ain't unhealthy. We all watched the way you ate tonight and drank that booze. I made a big dinner in the hope that we'd have leftovers. You ate everythan'."

"Hun, that's what you do when you're hungry."

"But, Lawrence, you no longer are doin' the diet the doctor said you gotta do."

"It was horseshit," he said, having a seat at the table.

"Please, get back on it. You got two little girls who wanna have a daddy. I can't afford anything happenin' to you."

"Susan, what you think is going to happen to me?"

"That ticker of yours will stop tickin'."

A pause.

"Please, Lawrence, go back on your diet. Lately, you've had me worried sick. I love you. I want you around for as long as I can. For the girls and me. Can you do that?" Susan begged.

* * *

Lawrence woke up to a stressful feeling around his heart—it was beating and beating so forcefully. Getting up from his bed, Lawrence made his way to the bathroom. He paused and tried to calm himself, but his heart kept on pounding. "Breathe, man, breathe," he urged. After some time, his body seemed to settle. Lawrence went downstairs and had a seat on the couch in the living room. As he did, he looked across at the clock on the wall. It read 11:22 pm.

Eventually convinced that his heart had relaxed a little, he threw on a pair of pants in the laundry room. In the main entrance, he slipped his jacket on and made his way out the door, heading to the bar around the corner. He had to be sneaky; Susan hated it when he went out drinking.

The bar was quiet when he arrived. He was already loaded from dinner, but Lawrence was a professional (most of the time) at being able to hide the drink in his system. He took a seat and proceeded to knock them back. One dark and three Ambers, two vodka tonics, and two whiskey shots later, the bartender approached. He knew Lawrence well, and he knew when to cut him off.

"Go home, Lawrence. You've been here for an hour just drinkin' and no talk."

"Give me one more," he said, but the bartender shook his head.

"Nah, my friend, I can't do that."

Lawrence frowned as he pulled out his wallet, laying it on the bar. He struggled to open it, pulling bills and coins out for another drink. "C-c-come, one more nah-nah-now," Lawrence slurred. The bartender stared at Lawrence as he wiped a glass clean in his hands.

"I'm sorry, friend, but no more."

"P-please, just give me one more w-whiskey tonic, then, then, I-I'll be gone," Lawrence slurred. But the bartender just shook his head 'no' while Lawrence shook his in disappointment.

Removing himself from the bar, Lawrence slid off his stool, doing what he could to keep himself up. Stumbling over to the door, Lawrence felt his world spin. Gliding his hand against the wall, he kept himself up and headed out.

"Hey, yo!" the bartender called out. Lawrence belched, then turning to the man, he saw the bartender walking over.

He handed Lawrence his wallet. "Almost forgot this, Lawrence. Need this, don't yeh?"

Lawrence glared at the man with a drunken frown. Snagging his wallet, he stuck it in his back pocket. Pointing a finger at the bartender, Lawrence burped, "I-I'm, not... Never mind."

Pushing the door open, Lawrence dragged his feet across the sidewalk. The night was calm, quiet, and only lit by the streetlights. They gave off a warm glow that irritated Lawrence in his drunken state, yet he knew he had to love them as they were his guiding light home. "Health"—*burp*—"is fine. Fuckin' fine," he mumbled as he stumbled. Lawrence then had the urge to take a drunken piss.

Cutting a corner of the sidewalk, Lawrence stood underneath a shrub that overgrew a backyard fence. There, Lawrence was sheltered. Taking a piss, he felt relieved. All was quiet in the night, with only his moaning and the sound of him peeing, until a voice popped up.

"Big L?" a recognizable voice said.

Lawrence, caught, turned away, snuck himself back into his pants, zipped up his fly, and struggled to do up his belt. A few feet ahead, two teenagers, students from the school he worked at, around the age of 14, stood by, catching Lawrence red-handed.

Lawrence let out an embarrassed drunken laugh. "W-what…you…doin'…up?"

"Little bit of public indecency, Big L. Been drinking a bit tonight?" the teenager asked with no true concern.

Lawrence let out a chuckle with a burp to follow.

"That's not polite. My name ain't… Big L," Lawrence said.

He then felt woozier as the cold night air became more noticeable, and he staggered from side to side.

"Big L. Drunk as hell," the first teenager said, smiling as he pulled out his phone and pointed the camera at him.

"D-don't. Put that away," Lawrence said.

Both the teenagers laughed, stepping closer to Lawrence, surrounding him, predator vs. prey. Lawrence, trying to keep his feet planted to the pavement, watched as both the kids stepped closer, laughing and mocking his drunkenness. He shook his head, raising his hand up, blocking the camera on the phone. "I-I said, p-put that thing... away." Yet the kids kept laughing, filming, and mocking him.

"Stop it!" Lawrence said, shoving the teen with the camera by the shoulder.

The kid took a few steps back, shocked at the sudden drunken rage that Lawrence displayed. The teenagers, still laughing, stood next to each other. The one with the phone was showing his friend the footage. Lawrence, fueled with rage, took a staggering step towards them and swatted at the phone in the kid's hand. He missed as the teens took a step back.

"Easy, Big L," the second teen said, slipping his hands into his pockets.

"Delete that now. D-delete it I—"

Lawrence then felt the rush of his insides bubbling up. His overindulgence in alcohol came rushing forth like a fountain, up his throat and out of his mouth. Lawrence aimed the vomit to drop near his feet. With shock and glee, the boys let out in hysterics, with the second friend taking his phone out to record this wonderful, drunken moment.

"You alright, chunky?" the first teen said with a laugh. With his hands on his knees as he bent over, Lawrence let out the last of his sickness. Wiping the bile from the corners of his mouth, he stood up, swaying as he did so, to turn and see both the boys aiming their phones at him with the flashlight blinding his sight.

"Yo! Big L, for a guy who's devoted his life to making the world clean, you're fucking filthy. Anything you want to say to the students of Glendale, sir?"

With a jolt of rage, Lawrence reached his left hand out and clasped onto the hood from the boy's sweater. Pulling the kid towards him, the boy's phone slipped from his hand and dropped into the pile of bile on the sidewalk. As he entered Lawrence's grasp, his feet slipped on the chunky mess, causing him to lose his balance and for Lawrence to grab hold of him.

"Let him go, bro!" his friend said, still filming.

"Stop filmin'. Leave m-me be."

The kid thrashed as he tried to escape his grasp, but Lawrence kept his grip tight. The friend, still filming, kept moving his body forwards and backwards, unsure of when to step in to help his friend or just keep filming the situation. While in Lawrence's hands, the young man began to let out a shrieking scream that echoed through the street.

"Let 'im go, man!" the friend cried out.

"Leave me be!" Lawrence begged.

The house to the right of them lit up from the commotion.

"Stop doin' what you doin'. Always pushin' me and pushin' me."

"Help me! "the kid cried.

Another house nearby lit up; the neighbours would soon come out. Lawrence, in a panic, shoved the boy away from him with all his strength. The young man stumbled in the direction of his friend. Slipping on the bile near his feet, he spun, landing on his back, cracking his skull on the pavement. The night went quiet, and the commotion came to a sudden halt. Lawrence stood still in shock. The second teen, camera in hand, stood near his friend, terrified. The boy on the pavement began to gasp for air. Lawrence, weak in the knees, took a shaky step closer and watched the boy, eyes wide and staring at the night sky, with blood pooling from the back of his skull down the cracks of the cold pavement.

"W-what did you do, man? What did you do?" the friend said, scared to even touch his pal.

Lawrence heard the creaking of the neighbour's screen door open to the right of him. A woman wrapping herself in a housecoat for warmth, stepped out to see what all the commotion was. Lawrence saw her, then brought his attention to the friend, standing beside his bloody buddy with tears in his eyes, raising his camera in Lawrence's direction.

"Help!" the friend cried out. "Help, this man attacked us!"

11

Phillip and Jesse were sitting on opposite couches in the basement when the lock slid upwards.

"Did you hear that?" Phillip asked. Jesse was with him, though he had his eyes shut and was in the middle of dozing off. Perking up, he saw how serious the kid was. Phillip was propped up in his seat, eyes sharp on Jesse.

He shook his head. "Nah, what was it?" Jesse asked.

Phillip waited a moment, then stood up. He thought about what the sound could have been, and then it hit him. "The lock!" he said, taking off upstairs. Jesse shook off the sleep in his head and joined Phillip in heading up the stairs.

"It's open!" Phillip yelled, and his voice travelled through the house. Grabbing the handle, Phillip twisted the knob, and opened the door. A cool, biting breeze trickled in, and it washed over both him and Jesse. It felt good. It tasted even better.

"Freedom, Freedom, freedom!" Phillip said, and Jesse nudged him.

"What did I say—just had to wait."

Darla, Floyd, and Lawrence came out of their rooms and headed toward the main entrance. As they did, they saw Ken pinned to the window, staring outside. Darla was curious about what he was looking at, but the excitement of the door opening was overbearing.

Phillip, arms stretched out, smiled at the crew and stepped outside. "Let's go home!" he shouted as he stepped out onto the front porch.

"Don't go out there!" Ken cried, almost begging. Stumbling, he charged towards the group at the door. As he came bolting, they couldn't understand why he was being the way he was. As he hopped down the steps, he began grabbing onto their shoulders and arms, pulling them away from the door.

Lawrence snapped his arm away. "Don't fuckin' touch me." He shoved Ken's shoulder.

"Something is out there. Something is in those woods," Ken warned, terror-stricken.

Phillip rolled his eyes and laughed. "You motherfucker. This guy wants us to stay. Shocker. Isn't it obvious now, guys? Ken here has had something to do with all this."

Darla and Floyd looked concerned. "What did you see, Ken?" Darla asked, but Ken struggled to come up with the words.

Lawrence chuckled. "Son of a bitch. He want us here. We're out. Game over, boy." As Lawrence made his way out, Ken grabbed him by both of his shoulders, pulling him backwards, but Lawrence didn't take this kindly. The big man spun, latched onto Ken's shirt, and pulled him close.

"You'll die out there," Ken warned.

Lawrence pulled him even closer, leaving them face to face. "You playin' a game, huh? It's over. We leavin'." Lawrence then shoved Ken against the wall.

"He's fucking playing," Jesse said and smirked.

Phillip waved. "Step on out, lady and gents. I'm gonna take off. Have fun at home." Giving a wink, he spun around theatrically and walked off the porch, heading towards the dark woods. The stars were out, giving the night a beautiful glow as Phillip gripped the front of his tux jacket, pulling the open ends close together. The cries begging for him to get back inside continued, but Phillip knew to ignore him, smiling as he did so.

Ken tried to push through again. "Someone stop him! Somebody is out there."

Lawrence, stepping onto the porch, turned around and said, "What the fuck you sayin'?"

"What did you see?" Darla asked again.

Robert scoffed. "This guy is nuts."

Thoughts ran through his mind, but Ken knew it was near impossible to explain it in a way they'd understand.

But, by God, he tried. "There was a lady, but there was something wrong. She had blood on her. All over her gown. Her face was gray, and it had deep cracks yet didn't bleed. This woman looked sick. Just upstairs, I saw her. Standing, kind of waving. She looked demonic, you know?"

They just stared at Ken, and then Jesse and Robert stepped closer.

"Get the fuck outta here," Lawrence said, rolling his eyes in disbelief.

"Ken, did you put us here?" Floyd asked.

"This seems like some kind of lazy attempt to freak us out," Robert said.

Ken shook his head furiously from side to side. "It-it smiled at me... Waved…"

Lawrence stepped off the porch but then turned around to Ken. "You're fuckin' full ah shit."

"If you go out there, you'll die. I saw it in her eyes!"

Lawrence entered the house and slammed the door shut as he targeted Ken. He raised a fist at him, but when the door closed, the lock slid horizontally, locking instantly. Lawrence froze while the others snapped their eyes to the sound, then back at Ken. "Holy shit," Jesse said in a panic, stepping over to the door, trying to open it. "No, no, no!" he cried.

"Jesus Christ," Darla said.

Robert seemed to be at a loss of words, as was Floyd. They both tried to help Jesse with the door, but it was now back to how it had been moments ago. Lawrence took a gander at what had just happened, then he lunged at Ken. "You knew!" Lawrence yelled as spit flew and landed on Ken's face.

"I-I didn't," Ken begged. Lawrence tossed him to the ground, and Ken landed on his side.

For what felt like the hundredth time, Darla tried to interject. "Wait," she said, yet Lawrence shoved her away, and she fell back against the wall. Lawrence, with great rage, clasped onto Ken's shirt.

Ken, defenceless on the ground, held his hands out to plead. "It wasn't me," he cried, but Lawrence drove his right fist into Ken's nose. Blood gushed and swung widely in webs as Lawrence crushed the bone on impact.

Phillip turned around when he heard the door shut. He just couldn't understand what all the fuss was about. "Suit yourself," he said, and he took off into the woods.

As Robert fiddled with the handle of the door, he caught the sight of Phillip, strolling into the darkness of the woods as it swallowed him whole. Then he was gone, and Robert knew, as did the rest, that he wasn't coming back in, and they weren't leaving.

* * *

Phillip walked on, slowly, making his way between the trees. They stood tall, scattered all around, and depending on how you looked at them, they appeared lined in rows—like military graves. Phillip heard and felt the wind blow gently. The tussling of the branches, and the crickets in the distance. Phillip shivered. Not just from the cold, but also from that feeling of fear brewing in his belly. He wasn't alone. *"It's just in your head,"* he thought. Ken had put fear in his mind. Phillip shook it off, kept himself together, and moved on. The farther he went from the house, the darker it became until the house was no longer visible.

* * *

Lawrence kept beating Ken—the man was like a beast unleashed. Darla cried, begging Lawrence to stop while Jesse and Robert kept at the door, struggling and screaming to open it. The room was chaotic. Floyd jumped onto Lawrence's back, pulling the man away from Ken, but Lawrence elbowed him in the stomach while he drove his punches, and Floyd, his breath taken away, landed on the floor, glasses clattering on the tile as he lay gasping for air.

"Please stop, Lawrence! Stop!" Darla begged, screaming with all her might. But even after this, Lawrence still gave Ken four more solid hits until he could no longer continue.

Ken slid to his side, his face bruised, bloody, and battered as he lay there, little gasps for breath coming in and out.

* * *

"*Phillip*," a soft voice whispered. He froze still, waiting, listening, sweating, terrified, and trying to hold his breath to hear anything near. He didn't want to believe he had heard it.

"Keep going," he said to himself.

After taking a few more steps, it came again. "Phillip…"

It was real, the voice, and not his imagination. It echoed from a distance, yet at the same time, it seemed like it was whispered in his ear. His head snapped towards the voice. Reaching his foot out, he took another step, his gaze rushing from left to right, but he saw nothing—only the trees and the darkness that blanketed them.

* * *

Darla hung over Ken, checking his breathing. "He needs help," she said.

Lawrence, out of breath, swung a kick between Ken's legs, and Ken only shook from the impact, unable to make a sound.

"Stop!" Darla shouted as Lawrence laughed and walked upstairs. As he made his way, he said, "Let the fucker die."

Floyd tossed his glasses on and got himself back up to his knees. Seeing the state of the beating, Floyd dry-heaved.

A mumbling rose from Ken's mouth, his face swollen and eyes sealed shut. Darla leaned in and listened. "Nahh…tt…me," Ken murmured.

* * *

Phillip walked up a little hill, not stopping, reminding himself that he was on his way home. That he would make it. All of this would soon be over. Climbing, he hoisted himself up by a small tree trunk. His sight was poor, and only the starlight cast down on the trees gave him guidance.

SNAP!

Phillip shot a look over to his right shoulder, hearing what sounded like the breaking of a branch. It wasn't in his head. Something was out there. His hands shook as he tightly squeezed and pulled on his pant leg. He wanted to make a clear-cut decision, but fear corroded his mind. Phillip stayed still for a moment. The only sounds he could hear were the gentle breeze making the branches dance and his heart beating through his chest.

"What the fuck are you thinking? Don't do it!" he thought, yet the words still came out running. "Hello? Anybody out there?"

Silence.

Phillip continued, "I was kidnapped and put in a house back there. I need help!"

Wind blowing. Branches scratching. Crickets echoing.

"Anyone? I know I'm not alone. I can feel you watching me. I won't hurt you."

He then noticed, standing in the darkness in the distance, a tree with the right half of a woman peering round, staring. "I see you," Phillip said.

"Phillip…" Another whispering voice came through, though this time from his left. He shot his eyes over, staring, but all he saw were trees. Bringing his eyes forward again, he set his sights to where the woman was just seconds ago, but she was gone. His stomach tightened; his breath seemed choppy as he tried to fill his lungs. All he wanted to do was run. So, he did. Back toward the house.

* * *

"Fuck!" Robert yelled, giving up on the door. Jesse soon followed suit, hands on his hips, squatting on the floor. Robert saw Ken and how Darla and Floyd were tending to him. It fuelled his anger. The man he now believed had a part in putting them here, was being helped by two of his captives. Robert stood by the basement steps, watching them lift Ken to his feet. "Why bother?" he asked, shaking his head.

Floyd shot him a look. "We don't know if it was him."

Robert spat at Floyd's feet. "Ignorant bastard." Then he went downstairs.

* * *

Phillip ran back down the hill, eyes up, hoping he was going in the right direction. As he ran, he felt the decline help him gain speed. It happened quickly—his foot catching a root sticking up from the ground—and Phillip took flight, soared briefly, and then he landed with a thud, toppling down the hill. His world spun for ten seconds until he finally stopped, landing with full force on his stomach and right hand. The pain of his now-broken wrist shot up his arm and into his back, and the first breath he took escaped him. It wasn't until he rolled on his back that his breath came back to him. *Go!* he thought.

Phillip pulled himself up like a drunken man, stumbling. Rolling his head, he shot a look in all directions. He'd lost his way. "Fuck! Fuck, fuck, fuck, fuck, fuck!"

"PHILLIP!" the voice screamed.

It came from behind him to his right, and his skin immediately broke out in gooseflesh. Holding his wrist tightly against his chest, Phillip started hightailing it towards where he hoped the house was. As he ran, the voice seemed to come closer—this time it was the voice of a little girl.

85

"You've killed, Phillip. You're a killer."

He kept running, and soon the voice came again, this time from his right—and close.

"What's wrong, Phillip. Are you scared?"

He turned towards the voice, yet he only saw trees flash past as he ran.

THUD.

Landing on his back, Phillip felt like he'd just been tackled like his old football days. He lay on his back, staring up, and saw stars. Raising his head, he looked at what was in front of him. Phillip, the genius that he was, quickly realized that he had run straight into a tree. His heart skipped a beat when he saw the woman in the bloody gown standing behind it, stiff as ever with her long black hair hanging in front of her face. Phillip stayed still for a moment, then, as quietly as he could, he pushed himself back, crawling on his elbows, not letting his eyes leave her as he rose on unsteady legs.

Phillip held his wrist close as he turned around to see another one, a little girl this time, dressed in an identical gown with an unworldly smile on her face. Phillip felt as if his heart had stopped. It was as if the devil's daughter was right before him.

* * *

Floyd and Darla dragged a stumbling Ken to Room 2. Laying him on his back, Darla went to the bathroom to grab one of the towels that were stacked neatly beside the bathtub. Jesse, while still at the door, stood, took a deep breath in, and tried to get himself together. "Tomorrow will be the night. Tomorrow will be the night. Just one sleep, and you'll be home. Just one sleep, and you'll be—"

BANG!

Jesse jumped as the crash erupted from behind, followed by a muffled scream. He spun around, still backing away. There he saw Phillip, slashed and bloody, crying and begging for his life on the other side of the vertical window. Phillip slammed his bloody hands against the glass, pleading as he sobbed, "Please! Let me in! Fucking let me in! Open it! Open it!"

Jesse stormed towards the door, grabbing the handle in a panic, trying to open it. He knew deep down that there was nothing he could do, but his adrenaline forced him to try.

Robert came rushing towards the chaos. He saw Phillip and went still, instantly in shock. Blood was smeared on the window like a splash of paint as Phillip pressed against the glass. Robert saw the slash across Phillip's chest, his tuxedo shirt soaked from his insides. Darla and Floyd rushed down the steps and saw the horrific scene outside. Darla's hands covered her mouth, and Floyd stood still in shock.

"Open it! Please, God! Please!" Phillip begged.

"I can't!" Jesse said as he struggled with the door. Darla went over to help, but Robert stood still, knowing that it wasn't going to open, horrified for his fate, nonetheless.

"We're trying!" Darla said as tears fell down her cheeks. Phillip rested his bloody, sweaty head against the glass, looking at Darla.

"They're coming. They're coming," Phillip said, sobbing.

"Who?" Darla asked.

"They're coming!" Phillip cried in terror.

Darla pulled on the handle, sharing space with Jesse so both could use their strength.

"Open the fucking door, Darla!" Phillip screamed.

"We can't…. We can't… We fucking can't!"

"Please ope—"

Arms wrapped around Phillip's chest, yanking him back. Those inside stepped away as it happened, and Phillip was thrown off the porch. Darla went straight to the window and looked past the smeared blood on the glass. Robert and Jesse couldn't see, and so they stepped on their toes to look over Darla's head, but it made no difference. Floyd ran up the stairs where he saw Lawrence watching out the window, and they stood beside one another until Robert and Jesse joined them.

Darla watched as what looked to be a mother and daughter tore at the flesh, ripping his guts from his body with razor-sharp talons. Phillip, with his last ounce of life, tried desperately, helplessly, to fight them off, but in a matter of seconds, he was being violently feasted on by the two creatures.

Darla stood still in disgust and terror, having to look away with an arm covering her mouth, crying and needing to vomit but finding herself unable to. After the sounds of bloody murder seemed to have settled outside, Darla heard steps slowly thumping on the porch. It stopped. Then, there was a gentle knock on the window. Darla turned around and saw the horrid woman, corpse-like in looks, with her skin cracked and gray. Her dark hair hung in front of her face, matted with Phillip's blood. Remnants of the gore ran from her mouth and dribbled down her chin. Her eyes were a dark, dirty yellow, peeking through the space between the bloody splatter on the window.

The woman stared at Darla, smiling with delight. She then began to laugh—the kind that sounded like a woman's, yet there remained a deep, horrid, coarse, whisky voice behind it. Then, she stepped away, grabbing a hold of Phillip's remains and dragging his body into the woods with the little girl skipping behind.

Darla stumbled almost drunkenly towards her room, using her hand to help guide her. Ken called out to her when she walked past, and his voice was faint, almost shadowed from the shock. Turning to him, Darla stood and looked, only really seeing his silhouette in the darkness of the room.

He spoke up again, "I... told you. I told you not...to...go out."

KEN

"This is what you gave me? This?" Ken's boss tossed a stack of papers on his desk, and they landed with a great thump. Ken, keeping his cool, raised his eyes from his desk and saw his boss—the slick-looking shit, arms crossed and furious—leaning against his cubicle wall. Ken leaned back in the office chair, staring at him for a moment.

"Would you like me to do them over again?" Ken asked.

"Hmm, let me think. No. Ken, this is the best shit you can give to this company. I think it's best we call it, don't you?"

"Call it? Wait, no. I'm retiring in a year."

"Well, congratulations, you just fast-tracked your way to getting out early."

"Please, listen, let me start the project again. Let me know what you'd like me to—"

"Don't worry; you're gone."

"Please, I—"

"Pack your shit, Ken, it's over."

An hour passed, and Ken was stood holding onto the box that contained the contents of his desk. It was time for the walk of shame. His heartbeat rose and stomach sank as he glared at the exit door. It stung, but he gripped his box, swallowed some courage, and took off toward the door, feeling all the eyes of his co-workers on him.

Ken was soon stuck in his car, the home traffic gridlocked. His mind raced with how he was going to tell his wife the news that the fucking weasel had fired him. The negativity of the day was weighing on his temper.

"Hey, fucker! Pull ahead!" a muffled voice said to him.

To the right of him was an angry driver, pissed at him for not moving fast enough. Ken rolled his eyes, cracked his neck, and tightened his hands on the wheel, crawling ahead through the traffic.

Flipping radio stations, there was nothing light. The news spoke of the latest scandal, then a possible new disease from China, the latest celebrity who couldn't stay faithful, and finally, a drug-related homicide. The music was no help either—every song felt as though it was nothing but about heartbreak.

Ken couldn't take it. "Fuck!" he screamed and slammed his fist against the radio, sick of the shit the day had brought him.

After two hours stuck in traffic, Ken finally pulled into his driveway. To make the day worse, the young next-door neighbour, a boy around twelve, was 'whipper snipping' the front yard of his parent's place, yet all the clippings were getting blown onto Ken's driveway. Ken got out of his car and stepped over to the boy. The young boy saw him and shut the whipper snipper off as Ken approached.

"Hey, buddy, I've told you before, that shit is not okay," Ken said, pointing to the mess on his property.

"I'm sorry, mister," the boy said with a frown.

"You're sorry? You were sorry last time. I told you not to do it, yet you do it again. What's the matter with you?"

The kid stood still, scared of Ken's rising temper.

"Are you deaf or something? Or are you just a dumb asshole?"

"I'm sorry."

"You said that already. What can I do to make you listen?"

"Ken!" a voice cried out.

He turned around and saw his wife, Hannah, standing on the front porch of their suburban home. She was mortified by the way Ken was speaking to the boy. Ken walked towards her, arms stretched out, shaking his head in furious anger.

"The kid doesn't listen," he muttered.

Hannah grabbed his arm. "You're blowing up again. Come inside, cool down, and we'll talk." Ken nodded his head, took a breath, and went to do just that as Hannah approached the young man and apologized for her husband's behaviour. As Ken stepped into the living room, he rested his hand against the wall, trying to calm himself. Hannah stepped up to him, crossing her arms.

"What was that?" she asked.

Ken took a moment. "Sorry," he said.

She was raising her eyebrows. "You're sorry. Yeah, I hope you are. The kid is thirteen years old."

"Well, fucking snowflakes these days need a little tough talk once in a while."

Hannah shook her head. "Yeah, just like you always got, and look how you turned out."

The whipper snipper outside roared again.

"That kid just makes a mess on our property when he does that."

"So, you speak to him politely, and if he does it again, you go and talk to the parents. Not cuss him out. What brought this on, Ken?"

Ken built the courage to tell her." They fired me today."

"Jesus, why?"

"That little shit was getting sick of me. Doesn't want any older people there, just young fresh faces. Ageism is what it is."

"Oh, Ken," Hannah said, pinching the bridge of her nose.

"I've let you down."

Taking a breath, she said, "Please, just go talk to the boy. Apologize."

"Apologize, no way. That will just allow him to keep doing what he's—"

'Apologize."

Shaking his head, Ken stormed past Hannah and out the front door. He stopped, and his anger built at the humiliation of what he would say to the boy while the kid continued snipping, having grass blow across the driveway. Ken's heart raced. He clenched his fist, counted to ten, and then headed over to the boy.

"Hey, hey," Ken said, but the noise from the whipper snipper was too loud, and the boy's back was to him. Ken let out a whistle. "Hey! Hey, kid!" he shouted, his frustration building. Ken reached over to tap him on the shoulder and get this over with, but as he did, the boy, not knowing he was there, turned around as the whipper snipper grazed both of Ken's legs, slashing them.

"Fuck!" he cried out from the sudden sharp pain.

Ken blew up, grabbing the young boy and tossed him on the lawn. As the boy landed on his back, Ken began to rain hell down on the poor boy's face, beating him to a pulp. His screams let out as he took the beating. Hannah heard some commotion above the noise of the rumbling whipper snipper that the kid still had slung around him. Yet Ken still had his hand gripped to the boy's shirt, beating the kid senseless. Hannah stormed outside, lunging herself on top of Ken, pulling him away from the boy, but it was as if she wasn't even there. His fists kept raining down until his rage defused.

12

Darla was kept awake all night by Ken's groans of pain. Even with the door closed, she could hear him as she lay on the bed and stared into the darkness. Eventually, Darla had to get up and move. She went to the living area, passing Ken's room. The sounds of his pain made her wince as she walked by, feeling horrible for his suffering. As she walked on, Darla entered the bright kitchen. The grumble in her stomach led her to the fridge, but she felt it wouldn't be right to take anything and not wait to eat with the others.

"Just wait a little longer," she muttered to herself. Turning around to head to the living room, that was when Darla saw it. An envelope was lying on the island counter. It was yellow with a happy face drawn in the middle with a blue pen. Someone could be here. Her thoughts ran wild, making her body shudder. Darla's eyes were automatically drawn to the door. Gulping down some spit, she took a look around the living room and kitchen. No one. Going down the steps and checking the mid-section, everything looked the same. The door was locked shut, and down in the basement, not a soul was present. The others were all still asleep in their beds.

As she went back to the kitchen, Darla grabbed the envelope. Shaking it, she both heard and felt the letter inside. With the nail of her index finger, she made a slit at the top. Hesitating at first, she tore the top off as quietly as she could, keeping her eyes on the hallway, hoping nobody could hear her. Once it was open, she looked inside and found a folded piece of paper, resting, waiting to be taken out and read. Darla hesitated again, then she took the paper out and unfolded it. Her heart raced.

It read:

Three days without water comes death at your door; have someone kick the bucket, you'll be thirsty no more.

It was a straightforward message to decipher, yet still, her head didn't want to understand. Folding up the empty envelope, she tucked it into her back pocket. She kept the letter in her right hand and re-read it three times. Not wanting to be the only one, she had to wake somebody. She trusted Floyd the most—the only other person who seemed to take action with reason. As she got to his door, Darla didn't bother knocking, opening it quietly and stepping in; she woke him. Floyd was only half-asleep anyway. He heard her as she entered, and he pushed himself up and moved away, ruthlessly paranoid.

"What?" Floyd said with a demanding whisper.

"I need to show you something," Darla said quietly.

"Show me what?"

"Just come look."

13

Glasses on and eyes focused. Floyd stood in the kitchen holding the letter, reading the simple message. In a whisper, Floyd asked, "You said it was just lying on the table?"

Darla nodded. "Yeah. Yellow envelope—sitting right over there. Had a smiling face on it, written in blue ink."

"What were you doing up?"

"I couldn't sleep."

"So, you chose to walk into the kitchen?"

"I was thinking of getting a bite to eat but then thought otherwise. That's when I saw the thing."

Floyd nodded, then looked back at the letter. "Those things got in here then."

"That's my guess."

"They want us to kill to get water. 'Kick bucket, be thirsty no longer.'"

"We can't do that."

"Kill? No, course not—you and me, at least. But one of our new housemates would," Floyd said.

"That's why I wanted to show you."

"You trust me the most?" Floyd asked after pausing, deep in thought.

Darla nodded.

"We keep this away from them. No way do they need to read this. Paranoia is already hitting those guys. They'll off Ken first," Floyd said.

"We wait for now. But there will be a point, if those doors don't open, that all of us will have to drink."

"I'll hide it for now." Floyd then opened his blazer and slipped the folded letter into the inner pocket.

14

By the time the sun had risen, Darla and Floyd had taken food out the refrigerator, made small, separate portions, and placed them on the table for the rest of the group. Darla ate her share of chicken right away, and food had never tasted better. She knew her body would crave more, but it was just another thing that she'd have to fight. Floyd had his as well, sighing with relief as he ate. "This tastes like both shit and heaven." Darla laughed, as did Floyd. A door in the hallway then echoed as it opened.

Stepping out was Robert, who didn't bother with a good morning. "Eating all our food?" he asked, eyes glaring.

"Of course not. I just made everyone a separate portion," Floyd said.

"This some fuckin' poor attempt to get on our good side?"

Shaking his head, Floyd said, "No, just eat the damn stuff if you want."

"Huh. I'll wait." Robert then went and sat down.

It wasn't long after that the others came out—except Ken. Jesse and Lawrence ate their portion right away. As they ate, Darla checked on Ken, who lay on his back, wheezing as his breath struggled in and out. Standing above him as he slept, Darla debated whether to wake him. Knowing he hadn't slept much, she left him be.

As she came back, she took a seat on the kitchen stool. There was only silence. The faces of the men showed they were all reflecting on the night before. Darla cleared her throat.

"I've got so much to look forward to when I get out. I'm a photographer, and I have two beautiful kids. I live in a great city, I've got a wonderful life, and I'm extremely fortunate." Darla stopped talking, waiting for someone else to continue.

Floyd smiled. "No kids, but I take care of my mother. I know I've mentioned that before, but what I didn't tell you all is that she has leukemia. It was a sudden thing. So, yeah, she needs my help. That's why I've got to leave."

The pair waited for someone, anyone, to join in.

Finally, Robert spoke up. "Business to run. A wife that hates me, and kids who don't really bother with me either. Really getting out of here because… well, I need to get the hell out."

Jesse spoke up next. "My guitar is at home. I miss it. My fingers are itching to pluck those strings. I haven't had a lot of gigs recently, and so I had to turn to teaching. After my daughter passed, my wife no longer had time for music. I used music many times to try and cheer her up, but it never worked. She needs me with her, so, that's my ticking clock."

"If you don't mind me asking, how'd she pass?" Darla asked.

Jesse paused for a moment. "Umm... suicide. Jumped in front of a bus. Bystanders reported that she went quickly. That's important." Jesse exhaled a breath, "That matters," he repeated.

"I'll miss good food if I stay cooped up in here. Kids I'll miss too, I guess." Lawrence let out a chuckle. "I guess my job ain't so bad. Don't love it. I'm a school janitor, so I'm always cleanin' up after them kids. Little shits sometimes, though. They call me 'Big L' for big loser. Many of them make jokes." Lawrence paused for a moment, looking down at the counter—not of sadness it seemed, but almost as if it were of remorse. He continued, "Anyway. Guess we'll all trust each other now?"

Darla smiled. "Trust. That's what we need right now. Trust in one another. It's the only way we can get out of this."

Jesse smiled. "You're not wrong."

Darla nodded and continued. "We've woken up in a—"

"Trust is essential," Jesse said, interrupting her.

The room fell quiet, and tension grew quickly like a virus in the silence. Robert tilted his head, sensing something was up, and Jesse stared at Darla and Floyd. His face was as still as stone. "Trust is all we have, and I love the fact that *you* are the one giving us a lecture on it." Jesse smiled. Darla awkwardly looked around the room, seeming nervous and tense. *He knows*, she thought.

Floyd picked up the same vibe of sarcasm from Jesse, hoping that his gut reaction was incorrect.

Robert panned around all of them. "Something up?"

Jesse ignored Robert's comment, laced his fingers together and leaned forward, keeping his unnerving smile, glaring at Darla and Floyd as if he were investigating them. "Should we trust both of you?" Jesse asked. Floyd took a breath, leaned his head up and straightened his back, ready for the impact of Jesse's soon to be words. "Of course, you can, Jesse. Of course, you can," Floyd said.

Jesse sniffed, keeping his smile, slowly dragging out his next words. "Is that right?" He then leaned back and crossed his arms. "Can I ask you two a question then?"

Darla and Floyd looked at one another, then back towards Jesse. "Shoot," Darla said.

"Good," Jesse said, keeping his piercing glare. "So… how come you two are keeping the envelope from us?"

Sweat began to form on Darla's forehead. She'd hate to admit it, but both of them began to display a masterclass on looking guilty. "Envelope?" Darla responded.

Robert swung his head between the standoff. "Envelope? What are you talking about?"

"There was an envelope on the kitchen table last night. I was up, saw it, then went back to bed. I didn't get much sleep, and I heard these two awake in the kitchen talking about it. Saying how they couldn't show us what it says."

Floyd raised his hand towards Jesse. "Look, we can exp—"

"What fucking envelope?" Robert interrupted, looking at both Darla and Floyd.

"There was an envelope left on the kitchen counter last night. We found it," Darla said.

"Well, why did you hide it from us?" Lawrence asked, stepping closer to the pair.

The room felt as if it were getting tighter. Darla and Floyd didn't even notice, but both of them slowly shifted closer to one another, soon finding themselves side by side. "Before we tell you what it says, please know that we only kept it from everyone because, well, we didn't feel it was right for us all to know what it said, considering what we all had just experienced," Floyd said.

"Cut the bullshit!" Robert shouted.

Darla and Floyd were silent. Floyd opened his blazer jacket and dug into his pocket to fish out the letter. Darla watched him do so, realizing they had no other choice. Floyd tossed the folded note on the kitchen table. It rested on the counter for only a half-second before Robert reached over and snapped it up. Unfolding the note, the others watched as his eyes panned wide as he read the poem.

Lawrence couldn't wait to find out what it had to say. "So?" he asked Robert.

Robert was crinkling up the paper as he held his glare on Darla and Floyd. "We can get water," he said, and Jesse and Lawrence immediately perked up.

"You were holding that from us?" Jesse questioned. "Why? To have it all to yourself?"

Robert shook his head. "Not just that, boys. The letter is saying someone has to die before we can get that water."

"We have to kill someone?" Jesse said.

"Look, we felt that right now, it wasn't a good time for us to do something that drastic for water. We could still figure out a way out of this place today," Floyd explained.

"But you kept this from us to hold that power. That knowledge. So, when the time comes, you can off one of us to get a drink," Robert said, folding up the paper and tossing it across the table. Jesse took the paper and gave it a read, then Lawrence took a glance right after. "We were cautious of Ken. We thought, the way things were going, one of you would, you know—"

"That's a hefty assumption," Robert told Floyd.

Floyd sighed. "Guys, I know this looks bad, bu—"

"It certainly does," Robert interrupted.

"Listen, it was because we didn't want anyone to do anything drastic so soon," Darla said.

Robert turned to Darla, his blood boiling. "You are something else. First, you call the shots, then you withhold information." Glancing over to Jesse and Lawrence, Robert gave a smile and a wink. "This is why we don't listen to dear sweet Darla," he said with a scumbag smirk.

"Oh, you little, little man," Darla said, using all her might to restrain her anger.

"It was a joint decision between us both, Robert," Floyd said.

Darla took a step towards Robert. Still doing what she could to remain calm, she approached him and spoke in a low tone. "Robert, this is not what you think. This wasn't against you guys. It was a choice we made that Floyd and I thought would help keep our minds clear so we could focus on our main objective."

"You think *you* can make the big choices?" Robert said to her in a seething, condescending tone.

"Enough, man," Floyd said to Robert.

"Enough? How desperate are you for her to get your rocks off?" Robert asked.

"Shut your mouth!" Darla shouted, slamming her hand on the table.

Her anger caused Robert and Lawrence to laugh; Jesse just stood watching the tension grow. "She can shout too. How about you do all the men in this room a favour—be a good little one and keep your voice down."

"Robert, don't push me!" Darla then looked away, shaking with rage.

"Keep your voice down, *Chocolate*," Robert sneered.

Darla turned back to him, eyes boring into him deeply. "What, did you call me?"

Robert motioned a kiss towards her, and Darla popped—he had gotten to her. She bolted towards him.

Floyd latched onto her arms and held her back from Robert, shouting, "He's not worth it!"

Darla thrashed in his arms, wanting to be set free, to get a piece of him. Robert stood at the other end of the kitchen, smiled, and gave Darla a wink. "I'm impressed by the lid on this one," Robert said. He laughed and headed downstairs.

"Bastard!" Darla shouted after him. All her fear and frustration and anger built up. Like a champagne bottle on New Year's, she was shaken to the core, then popped. Tears flowed as she continued to try and get herself out of Floyd's grip.

He held her as tightly as he could, repeating the same words to her: "It's not worth it, Darla. It's not worth it." A couple of minutes after Robert left, Darla seemed to settle. Still ravished with rage and shaking nerves, she was finally let go. She stormed off to be alone. Floyd took a breath with Lawrence and Jesse—both seemed to almost enjoy the spectacle.

15

9:00 pm struck and Lawrence, Jesse, and Robert stood by the door, watching the lock slide north. They waited, feeling the air trickle inside. The night was just like the last—no rain, only stars and a gentle breeze.

"It is 9:00 pm on the dot. Just like I thought," Jesse said, staring at the clock. With the door open, they waited, knives from the kitchen in each hand. Lawrence had one, and Jesse had two—as did Robert. Out of the seven of them, Darla and Floyd had snagged theirs earlier. They had one each. Only the three guys were standing by the door. Both had stayed in Ken's room, guarding him from the other men. Instead of going straight for the kill, the guys chose to open the door and wait for the mother and daughter. That's what they called them at least, not knowing if that was even a fact.

The door was fully propped open, but none of them stepped out. After the events in the kitchen, they felt like a team, but none truly deep down trusted any other enough to go past that door. They all waited inside. "What if we keep the door open, but only a crack, then we take off in the morning when there's light?" Jesse said, slightly gleaming from his idea.

"I like it," Robert said, and Lawrence gave a nod of agreement. Gently pushing the door to, they kept it open a sliver. "We need to stand here and keep guard. Do it in shifts. Two hours, then switch," Robert said, and they all smiled in agreement.

"I'll wait first," Lawrence offered, and the others took him up on it.

"Keep them eyes peeled. I'll watch from the window," Robert said.

Darla sat against the bed frame in Room 2 beside Ken. Floyd sat near Ken's feet at the end, tossing his knife back and forth across each knee. "I can't believe we didn't grab all the blades," Floyd said.

"If we had, they would have ambushed us for them," Darla whispered.

Ken let out a groan.

Darla leaned over. "Ken, nod if you can hear me."

He nodded.

"Can you speak?"

He spoke, but only faintly. The words that came out were muffled.

"Damn," Floyd muttered, shaking his head at the state of the poor man.

"One of us has to watch him at all times tonight," Darla said, and Floyd nodded his head in agreement. As he did, he felt that dehydrated headache echo around his head. It reminded him of his dry throat as he tried to swallow.

Darla spoke of her headaches. They rushed in and out at times, but her dry tongue was what bothered her the most. As she shut her eyes, thoughts of her favourite pop commercials came to mind. Darla chuckled as to why that would be; she hardly drank soda. Maybe that was why.

As Lawrence stood by the window, he caught the silhouette of the woman by the trees. Rubbing his eyes, Lawrence wasn't sure if it was his mind beginning to crack or if it was indeed that creature. Looking closer through the vertical window, he focused again. He must have been going crazy. No woman was in sight.

"Did you see that?" Lawrence called out to Robert.

While sitting on the couch that was nearest the window, Robert had been dozing off. The lack of sleep, water, and overall paranoia was getting to them. Once Robert heard Lawrence's voice, his head sprang up like a hungry hen's. His eyes darted at the deep, dark woods, but he couldn't make anything out.

"Nah, nothin'," Robert called from the living room.

Lawrence kept his eyes on the woods, and minutes passed with nothing. While Lawrence stared, his eyes were gaining weight, fluttering. When his eyes slid shut for a moment, Lawrence caught himself, bringing his head back. He whacked himself with his clenched fist that had his blade in hand. "Keep 'em open, dumbass," he begged himself. His eyes then caught movement again. This time the movement came to the right of his view. With his left hand, Lawrence clasped the door handle, readying himself to shut it. The little girl stepped out of the woods, standing in her nightgown, looking as hellish in the distance as she did up close.

"I see that!" Robert called out before Lawrence could ask, and Robert's voice startled him when he spoke. Robert rushed down the stairs, and Jesse woke up from the couch and got to the window to overlook at what he thought was the Devil's daughter.

The little girl, gracefully, in small, slow strides, walked towards the house. This small, white figure approached from the big, dark, and scary woods, growing a little more significant as she made her way towards them.

Robert and Lawrence stared at her, both squeezing closer to one another. Their eyes no longer felt heavy with tiredness but were now wide open with fear. Robert was to the left side of Lawrence. He pressed between Lawrence's huge body and the wall to the right as they watched the young girl approach. Slow, graceful strides—mastering the art of being terrifying. This apple did not fall far from the tree.

"They know when it's open," Robert said.

Lawrence took in a nervous breath. "Always waitin', always—"

"Watching," Robert finished.

"Come out and play," the little girl said gently.

Then silence.

The men, eyes pinning the girl, stared, frozen to the spot.

A screeching, nerve-shattering, stomach-knotting scream echoed into the night sky. It erupted from inside the woods and came barrelling towards the house. No matter where they were, everyone heard the screeching, animalistic cry of death rip through. The little girl ran towards the door at an unnatural speed. Robert pushed it closed, and the lock slid sideways, sealing the door for the night. When it did, the girl came to a full-stop, standing still. She let out a cry that could burst ear drums and shatter glass. Everyone immediately covered their ears to protect themselves from the horrid noise.

"Jesus Christ!" Floyd said, stumbling out of the bedroom and heading toward the living room.

The cry stopped, followed by a sudden silence.

"What the fuck is going on?" Floyd shouted in the now-quiet house.

None of the men said anything. They watched as the woman walked over to her daughter. Holding onto her hand,

and waving at them in the house, she took off back into the woods.

.

16

Darla and Floyd sat on the floor with their backs to the edge of the bed. Ken lay above them, his groans letting out. Darla sat, eyes glaring at the closed door in front of her, and a lone tear ran down her cheek. "I just want to see my babies again," she said in a whisper.

Floyd turned to her and rested his right hand on her neck. "Hey, you will. It won't be much longer, I'm sure of it. There's a reason why we're here, and we'll get that answer soon," Floyd said, smiling at her.

Ken let out another moan—this time with words seeming to escape. Darla got to her knees and leaned over him, gently touching his forehead. Softly, she asked, "What was that, Ken?"

He heard what she said, resting his palm on her cheek. Taking in a wheezy breath, he said, "It...h-hurts...so...m-m-much." After Ken finished, he licked his lips, flaky from dehydration, the blood in his mouth sticky.

Darla smiled in what she hoped was a reassuring way. "We'll get you help as soon as we can." She wanted to believe that, as did Floyd, but both had that uncomfortable truth resting in their bellies. Both knew Ken wasn't going to last. From his looks, he had maybe a couple more days.

Darla slumped down beside Floyd again, but he could see her trying to hide her emotion. Bringing her hands in front, she felt only a small amount of wetness from her eyes on her palms. Her body was unable to produce the normal amount due to dehydration. Darla, hesitating at first, eventually brought her hands to her mouth, licking up what she could.

"It's salty," Floyd said as she clenched her palms once.

Darla laid her head back. "So… thirsty. I could—"

"Kill for a glass of water?" Floyd said.

A silence of realization came after. "That's what they want. That's exactly what they want," Darla said. Floyd nudged Darla on the shoulder. Leaning in, he whispered, "We can't let these people win. If we protest, maybe we all can get out of here sooner. Make this game boring to them. Besides, I'm sure we can last another two days."

Darla paused for a moment, then turned to Floyd. "Think Robert or Lawrence would take out Jesse? I get this feeling that both aren't actually a fan of him."

Floyd tilted his head from side to side in that 'maybe' way of his. "I doubt it. All three would rather go through us and get Ken here. He's made enemies out of Robert and Lawrence more than that lazy fuck Jesse has managed."

"There will come a time, Floyd, when we will need a drink."

"'Til then, we try and find an alternative—like getting out of here. I don't want blood on your hands or mine. You and I agree we'd hate to see bloodshed in this house. Instead, we keep our focus first on finding a way out. This is a man-made structure; there have to be flaws."

"But what if it isn't? We've got two things out there in the woods I'd never call human. Floyd, this very well might be something that only mimics."

"Mimics?" Floyd asked.

"Yeah, like its own interpretation of what it thinks a house is like. Have you ever been in a house where everything is made only to look real? No light switches on the wall. All that shit. Nah, I don't think you have."

"It can't be supernatural," Floyd said.

"Why not?"

Floyd broke his whisper, raising his voice. "Because it can't. That shit isn't real."

"Lower your voice," Darla asked.

Floyd took in a breath, pinching the bridge of his nose again." I'm sorry, I just don't have time to believe in the supernatural."

"From what I saw out there, Floyd, we better start to."

"I can't. I won't." Floyd then stood up with his blade still in hand. "We will stay up in shifts to watch over him. In case we both fall asleep, I think one should stay inside, leaning against the door, and one should be in the living room." Darla nodded. Floyd then went to the door, stepping over Darla's legs. "I'll see you soon," Floyd said, then he left.

Closing the door behind him, Floyd walked towards the end of the hallway. The closer he got to the kitchen, the more searing bright light stung his eyes, causing him to squint as he stepped closer. He cut the corner, and Floyd felt hands shove him, strong enough to lift him off his feet and cause him to land on his side. His knife left his hand and clattered on the floor. Floyd turned and saw that it was Lawrence that had pushed him. Reaching over, Floyd grabbed the knife and pushed himself towards the kitchen with his feet, keeping his blade aimed at Lawrence.

"What is wrong with you?!" Floyd said with a mixture of anger and terror.

Lawrence took a step closer, his gleaming smile more prevalent the closer he stood under that kitchen light. "You can't watch that Kenny-boy for long. He's gotta go soon. No drink and we all die. You both ain't guardin' him forever." Floyd kept pushing himself back until he had enough room to stand. When he did, Floyd kept the blade aimed at Lawrence. "Make the smart move. We don't want to kill both y'all to get to him. Hell, none of us would want a little fight to break out. That'd be fun for nobody," he said sarcastically.

"Fuck you all," Floyd said with the spit of his own mouth strung out to his chin.

Lawrence saw the saliva. "Bettah save that. Gonna need it." Lawrence then turned around and headed downstairs. Floyd kept watching him as the big man made his way, but he was unsure what Lawrence meant—that was until the coolness on his chin made him realize. Floyd quickly wiped it away, more out of embarrassment than disgust.

17

Floyd was resting against the door in Room 2, doing what he could to keep his eyes open—Ken's snores oddly made him sleepier. His eyes felt heavy, sometimes even snapping shut. Floyd would then whip his head back, waking himself as his head felt like it was falling. He'd rub his forehead, take deep breaths, and even smack himself across the face. Floyd would have thought the nerves from the men downstairs would keep him up, but they weren't. He began to doze off again, slumping his chin down to his chest, his world becoming black.

"Shhaa."

Floyd woke to attention. It was the first voice he'd heard in hours. His eyes daggered to Ken's silhouette. The cry escaped from it as it travelled to his ears.

"Shiiiiit," Ken muttered. Floyd stood to attention.

"What is it?" Floyd asked, but Ken didn't respond; only then, Floyd saw that he was trying his best to sit up.

"Baa-ttthhhrooom," Ken moaned.

Floyd nodded with realization. "Oh, OK, alright. One sec."

Opening the door slowly, Floyd stuck his head out, checking if the hallway was clear. The doors had all been shut. Floyd turned back around, reaching over and lifting him by the arm. "We have to be quiet, OK?" but Ken didn't respond. Only his breath against Floyd's ear let him know he was still battling.

Stepping out of the room, Floyd slowly shuffled Ken toward the bathroom with one arm around him and the other keeping the knife tight in his grip and ready.

Once inside, Floyd brought Ken to the toilet. Reaching his foot out, Floyd lifted the lid with the toe of his shoe, tossing it up. Ken, in a drunken way, unbuckled his pants and slid them down awkwardly. Floyd winced in the dark bathroom only lit through the skylight. Keeping his eyes up not to see anything, Floyd lowered Ken down to the seat. Once he did, Floyd turned around. "I-I... m-ay....be...a while," Ken said softly.

This guy, Floyd thought as he rolled his eyes. "Alright. I'll be right here." Floyd then stood over in the corner.

"Y-you watchin' me? Get out," Ken said. Floyd shook his head and left the bathroom, standing out in the hallway, waiting. Time passed, and Floyd was getting worried. Having a seat against the wall, he gave Ken five more minutes. While staying put, he saw Darla sitting on the couch in the living room, sleeping peacefully. Floyd smiled, his eyes feeling heavy. Giving in to their weight, he fell into the darkness.

18

Ken, staggering slowly, made it back to his room by himself. He got comfortable in his bed, falling asleep straight away. The room was in utter silence for the next half-hour until there was a small clatter. He awoke, unable to move his eyes. Ken knew who it was—just a shift change. Darla, he guessed by the steps. Ken understood why they watched over him, but the concussion was making his mind loop. Ideas and thoughts ran in and out. Some seemed true, only for him to realize later that they weren't. At times, he thought he heard things, felt things that ended up not being real. Like being half asleep yet *really* fully awake. But even in his state, Ken realized he didn't have long. Whatever damage was done by that bastard Lawrence, it was fatal.

His hand covered his mouth, but only seconds after he realized it wasn't his own but *someone else's*. A second later, a blade tore through his chest and dug deep. Ken was in a world of pain and darkness, struggling to breathe while striving to push his assailant away.

Thrashing his arms towards his attacker, Ken did all that he could to go out with a fight. But the attacker had pinned both his arms down. Ken struggled for air but couldn't catch any. He felt his blood running past his breastplate and down his sides, soaking into the sheets he lay on. The blade left his chest, and Ken's body lifted with it, then he flopped back down once the knife was out. Right away, the knife drove straight under his bellybutton, twisting, and Ken moaned in pain. The knife escaped his body again, landing on the right side of his neck.

19

Opening her eyes, everything was a blur. Each blink felt dry. This had to have been the worst sleep yet. It was then, when Darla turned her head, that her eyes found the kitchen. Sitting on the countertop near the sink were two large jugs of water, with five glasses next to them. Her first reaction was excitement until the reality set in.

Darla stood up to see Floyd lying on the floor. Her heart beat so quick it hurt. Running over to him, she got down to her knees to see if he was alright. His face was bloody, and his glasses lay on the floor next to him. With both hands on his cheeks, Darla shook him awake. "Floyd! Wake up, Floyd!"

And he did so, but he was clearly in a daze. He woke up like he didn't know what had hit him. He sat there mumbling. Darla didn't bother deciphering what he'd said, but instead, in a panic, she rushed into Room 2.

The light from the window cast an almost beautiful glow on Ken as he lay on his back, eyes open, facing the ceiling, drenched in his own bloody mess. Covering her mouth, trying not to retch, Darla took a half-step forward to see the cause of death. *Who the hell did this?* she thought. Multiple stab wounds—chest, stomach, and neck—all leaving bloody trails.

"Good riddance," a voice over her shoulder said, and Darla spun around to see Robert standing in the doorway, glaring at the body.

ROBERT

The room was dark other than the light coming from the hockey game on the TV, and the crowd roared as the home team scored. Robert swung his fist in celebration. Taking his beer, he ventured a celebratory sip. He rested the beer down and clapped after, happy as he could be with the home team's goal giving them the lead. With his eyes fixated on the game, he didn't hear his wife, Mia, sobbing and speaking to him in her soft, emotionally damaged tone. What Robert did hear was the click of the hammer pulled back on his pistol. The click was one Robert knew too well. His body went tense; both he and Mia didn't say anything, the only sounds in the room coming from the cheers of the crowds on television.

Robert turned to see his wife, hands shaking with fright, mascara and tears running down her cheeks, aiming the pistol at him with both hands. Robert, eyes planted tensely on Mia, kept still with both his hands planted on each arm of the chair. Mia took a step towards him with her face now aching with despair. She cried with tremendous disgust and rage. Robert leaned forward in the chair, and with slow, gentle movement, he raised his hands slightly above his head.

"Hun, what the hell are you doing?"

Mia didn't speak; she sobbed, keeping the pistol aimed as best she could. Robert could see she wanted to talk, and at this moment, no words could come from her.

"Hun, please, lower the gun. Lower the weapon—"

Her voice was soft with emotion, but she managed to speak above her tears. "You're a pig," she said, taking a stride closer. Robert leaned back as he watched the unsteady barrel of a pistol wave directly at him.

"If you lower the gun, w-we can talk. We'll talk, sweetheart," Robert said, his voice now trembled.

Mia shook her head. "No, No. You won't get away with this. Y-you won't."

"Mia, lower the—"

"YOU WON'T GET AWAY WITH THIS!"

Robert held his tense glare. Mia wiped some of her tears away with her right arm, doing so with a quick swipe on her sleeve, still keeping the pistol pointed. With his hands still held in the air, Robert, with caution, stood from his chair.

"Sit down," Mia said.

"Let's talk."

"SIT DOWN!" Mia screamed, her shrieking voice cutting like a knife into Robert's guts.

Robert sat straight back down, arms still in the air.

"Oh-okay, Okay. Babe, I'm listening. Please, just… j-just talk to me, talk to me, okay?" Robert said.

Mia, now hyperventilating, forced words past her sobs.

"You're a pig. A filthy animal."

Robert tilted his head with an inclination of what she was talking about.

"I think you—"

"Abby," Mia said, aiming the shaky pistol just a nudge closer.

Robert's heart stung when he heard the name. He kept his eyes on Mia and tried smiling to calm her down. Bringing his left hand towards her, he brought his palm face up.

"Give me the gun, dear. I'll explain everything. It's not what you—"

"I know exactly what it is."

There was a pause.

"Mia, please, le—"

"And Jessica. And Louise."

Robert sat back in his chair. Mia watched him sweat now. He had no words. A smile broke from her scrunched, sobbing face. Robert sat there, still, lowering his hands and resting them on the arms of the chair. A goal was scored in the hockey game, and the music and air horns and joyful cheers broke from the crowd, but Mia and Robert kept their eyes on one another.

"I called them," Mia said.

Robert shook his head and said, "Mia, you should have let me explain."

Her head shook. "Explain? E-explain what? You're a monster. A pervert. You are scum."

"Who did you call?" Robert asked with a tremble in his voice, now more robust.

"The police are coming."

"FUCK!" Robert cried out. He stood out of his chair, and as he did, Mia stepped back, the pistol now pointed at his chest. "Mia, I have to run. I have to go. Please, please don't shoot me, I have to run. I'll explain all of this later. I promise, sweetheart, this is all a mistake.

"I am not letting you out of this house," Mia said.

Robert raised his hands in the air, with tears streaking down his cheeks. "P-put the gun away, dear, please. Let me go, let me go, and I'll explain everything once it's cooled down."

Mia shook her head slowly, left to right. "I found the texts, all of them. All those poor girls you were trying to entice."

Robert took slow steps towards Mia, and as he did, Mia followed each step as she shuffled back with the still pistol aimed. Robert, arms out, begged her with his pleading words, "Look, none were fruitful, and I know it's terrible. I have a problem—okay, I know that. But please, let me leave before they show, and I'll explain everything later."

"Thirteen-year-old girls, you pig. You pig. You disgusting animal!" Mia cried, wanting to retch from the sickness of the words that escaped her.

Wisps of blue and red light came from the window, lighting up the dimly lit living room. Robert turned to see the police cruisers had now arrived to take him away. "You're a monster," Mia said again, and Robert brought his attention back to her.

'Jesus, oh no. Oh, God, no. I have to leave. I have to—"

"You are not going anywhere!" she shouted.

Robert's head kept snapping back from the window to Mia. With her sights past her pistol, she watched as the man she once loved melted as his shameful crimes were brought to the surface. She hadn't a clue Robert had this in him in all the years she had known him. It was a nightmare coming true.

"Step aside," Robert demanded.

But Mia refused. "No. You're done. D-done."

Robert kept his eyes pinned on her. There was silence between them, with only the noise of skates carrying players across the ice. Mia watched the way Robert kept his eyes on her. Her heart was beating. The weight of the gun and the sweat from her palms kept it a challenge holding the pistol. Robert took a breath, then gave his final plea.

"Mia, I love you. I love the kids. Don't do this. What you have done is a mistake. You don't want to cause our marriage to crumble and our family to break apart, do you?"

"Stop it," Mia said.

"If you don't let me through, you'll be the cause of us being a broken family. Do you want that, Mia? Is that what you want? That's what your actions will do,"

"Shut up!" Mia cried.

"Step aside, dear."

"No."

"Hun, step aside, now."

"I won't. You deserve hell. You deserve—"

"Lower the gun, Mia, and step aside!" Robert shouted.

"I won't!" Mia shouted back.

"They'll catch me, Mia, and I'll go to jail for the rest of my life. They'll kill me in there. Kill me. Now put the gun down. Put it down, Mia, for fuck's sake!"

"No," Mia said with a tidal wave of tears.

"Mia, please. Please, I beg you," Robert said.

Mia kept the pistol aimed and shook her head. Robert brought his attention back to the window. The police officers were already exiting their vehicles. Robert turned around, glared at Mia, and bolted towards her to get past. And when he did, the trigger was pulled.

20

Darla was frozen, unable to move. At first, she couldn't think of what to do.

Floyd walked over with his hand on his head. Once he saw the body, his eyes went wide. That was when Darla came snapping at him. "What happened?" she asked him.

He mumbled at first, doing what he could to muscle up a sentence. "I-I fell asleep. I woke up when I felt someone grab my shirt. But just as I was about to open my eyes, I was attacked. That's the last thing I remember."

Darla stormed over to the kitchen. Robert stood, pouring himself a glass of delicious water, and Darla walked up behind him. "Did you do it?" she asked, but Robert didn't even bother turning around, let alone give a response. He lifted the glass to his lips and took the first sip he'd had for days. "Did you do it?" Darla demanded.

Once he had downed his drink, Robert exhaled and smacked his lips. "Us humans have made all sorts of drinks.

But nothing beats natural water. Nothing." He then turned around and smiled at Darla, stroking his beard.

"You monster. You fucking monster," she said, misty-eyed.

"Drink up, sweetheart, before it's all gone," Robert said, smiling with a wink.

Darla took a few steps forward. "How could you?"

Robert's eyes looked past Darla, and he smiled. Behind her stood Jesse. He looked as though he also shared a terrible night's sleep. His eyes lit up at the sight of the water.

"Thank God," he said as he shuffled past Darla.

Her gaze followed him as she asked, "Was it you? Did you all have a part of this?"

As Jesse poured himself a glass, he turned to her and shrugged. "Don't know what you're saying."

Darla knew they had both had something to do with it. Jesse was a lazy human and an even lazier liar. "Ken is dead."

"And what's the problem?" Robert asked, keeping that smile.

Darla took a breath. "The problem is we have now lost control. We've given them what they want, and now they know they have us by the throat."

Robert chuckled and shook his head, "Darla, dear. We have to drink to survive."

"A man has been made a sacrifice, and it's only been two nights!"

"By the third, we could be out and on our way," Robert said.

At that point, Floyd stepped out of the hallway and saw the water on the counter. "Jesus, when did that show-up?"

But nobody answered his question.

"Do you know what this means? Do you know what this shows?" Darla asked, getting closer and closer to Robert. "It shows, Robert, that we are willing to kill. To actually kill a person. Our trust level here is now at zero, Robert, because you killed him."

Robert smiled, leaned over, and grabbed a glass for Darla. He held it before her as she struggled to understand.

"What makes you think I killed him? Huh? Just drink the water, *Chocolate*."

The room erupted in violence. Darla smacked the glass from Robert's hand, sending it soaring and crashing into pieces. Clasping onto his beard, Darla tugged his head down and gave him a wallop with her free hand. Jesse stood out of the way, and Floyd jolted head-on into the action. Darla gave four of the best shots that she could manage before Floyd pulled her away, and Robert shoved her. Red-faced and furious, Robert, like a bull, got right into her face.

"You fucking bitch!" he spat.

"You murderer!" Darla responded, thrashing and trying to free herself from Floyd's grip.

"Enough!" Floyd yelled.

"Come on, come and get me. Come on.!" Robert said, egging her on.

"You miserable piece of shit! He was defenceless! Fucking defenceless!" Darla cried out. Floyd then backed up and tossed her towards the living room. She stumbled, turned around, and charged at Robert again, with Floyd now jumping between both with his arms up, doing what he could to stop the fight as they attempted to tear each other apart.

"Be grateful, and drink your fuckin' water!" Robert hollered.

Floyd turned around, jumping in front of Robert. "Stop this. Stop it right—"

Swinging his fist, Robert struck Floyd in the stomach, stealing his breath. Dropping to one knee, Floyd clenched his stomach, and his glasses dropped to the floor.

Darla swung one leg over the top of Floyd, jolting towards Robert. She swung a punch, but Robert caught it. The scrap led them to where the hallway and living room met, and Robert body-checked Darla to the floor with his left shoulder. As she lifted her head, Darla saw him stepping towards her, gaining momentum. He swung his foot, kicking her across the mouth.

The living room fell silent.

Floyd looked up, seeing only a blurry silhouette of Robert. Darla was out cold and lying on the floor. Lawrence walked up from the hallway behind Robert, while Jesse came around the corner behind Floyd. All three were looking down at him. Floyd kept his hand on his stomach as nauseating pain surged through him. He rolled his head around and glared at all of them. "Didn't take too long for you all to become animals, did it?" he said, shaking his head.

Robert stepped over to him, still keeping his eyes on Floyd and said, "Lawrence, man, water's on the table."

Floyd watched the blurry form of Lawrence turn and head over to the water. "Good stuff," Lawrence said.

Floyd started to stand, but Robert was quick to shove him back down. Clasping on to his shirt, he pulled Floyd close and spoke into his ear, "Listen, you and the bitch are done playing games. And I mean fuckin' done. From now on, I'm in charge. Comprendre?"

Floyd didn't respond, and Robert disgustingly built up a loogy and spat it on Floyd's face. His left eye took the hit, temporarily adding to his blurry vision as he rubbed it away.

As Floyd wiped his eye, Robert said, "Can't see?" then he brought his foot down on Floyd's glasses, smashing the left lens to bits and cracking the other. "Let's keep it that way."

21

"Darla, Darla, hey, wake up." The voice was faint. She then felt her body shake. "Darla, can you hear me?"

Her eyes opened, and there, above her, was Floyd, smiling with relief as she looked up at him. Darla sat up in a bed that Floyd must have brought her to. She wasn't sure which bedroom was hers—they all looked the same. A headache rushed in, but Floyd had a glass of water with him. Helping her sit, he reached over and handed her the glass. Taking it, she took a sip. It felt like heaven.

"They're leaving," Floyd said with a big, gleaming smile.

Darla was confused. "Who?"

"Robert and Lawrence."

Darla felt a good chunk of stress leave her body. Hand shaking, she took another sip. After, Darla placed the cold glass on the right side of her cheek where her bruise was. Her skin had swollen.

"How much pain are you in?" Floyd asked. Taking a moment, then raising her head, she said, "Too much." Lifting the glass, she then drank the rest and gave it to Floyd before swinging her feet off the bed.

Resting her feet on the floor, she took notice of the night sky from the window. She was surprised at how long she must have been out. "How long was I asleep?" she asked.

Floyd thought for a moment. "Give or take...all day." He laughed. The room was dark, but because of the starlight, she was able to see him.

"Where are your glasses?" she asked, and Floyd looked down in disappointment.

Slipping them out of his blazer, he reached over and showed her the smashed eye-wear in the palm of his hand. "Robert," he said. "Robert did this."

Darla shook her head. "Of course, he did."

22

Lawrence had a pillowcase open, taking rations for their trip. Oddly, he and Robert were fair, taking only what they thought they would need. Each knocked back two glasses of water, then tied up their pillowcase stuffed with food, with Lawrence swinging it over his shoulder. They held a knife in each hand, and both moved to the basement and stood wait by the door. Jesse, Darla, and Floyd watched the clock. "Good luck out there. Send help," Darla said.

Robert turned to her, making kissy lips. When he was done, he gave a chuckle. "Right. I'd juuuust love to be your hero."

The clock was approaching 9:00 pm—there were about thirty seconds to go—and Robert turned to Darla and Floyd, smiling. He walked over to the last step of the mid-section staircase, stroking his beard with a smile. "You aren't going to last much longer here. So, really, I should say good luck to you."

Lawrence walked over and joined him, also smiling. "Goin' to kill them bitches. Pave the way for y'all."

Darla gave a wink. "I hope you do."

Suddenly, footsteps were heard running on the porch outside, then there was a slam against the door. It was followed by screams and a vicious thunder of fists, begging to get in. It startled everyone out of their skin. A man in a bloody white shirt and black pants, missing a shoe, begged for the door to be opened. "Please let me in! Please!" the stranger cried in hysterics.

Robert and Lawrence turned, with the sack of food dropping to the floor. Both now pressed against the back wall. "Who the fuck is this guy?" Robert whimpered.

Darla and Floyd rushed down the steps and stood in front of the door. He was being chased. Darla could see the woman and the little girl running towards him as they left the woods.

"Don't let him in!" Robert demanded.

The lock then slid up. 9:00 pm on the nose. Darla swung the door open, and the stranger toppled in. She slammed the door just as the two hunting him were about to hit the porch. The lock slid sideways, sealing the door shut right away. The stranger crawled across the floor as Robert thrashed his head back and forth toward the man and Darla.

"How could you let him in? Huh, fucking bitch?" Robert asked, angered beyond limits. The stranger held his bloody arm to his chest, sweaty and crying. The man had looked as though he'd been through hell and back.

23

The stranger sat on the couch with his injured arm wrapped in a bathroom towel pressed against his chest. He sat with his eyes pointed to the floor, shaking like a convulsing dog. The group stood surrounding him. All eyes were on the visitor. "While I was wrapping your arm up, you said your name was Martin, right?" Darla asked. The man unglued his gaze from the floor, then stared at her as she sat down, keeping a distance on the left side of the couch. He only nodded a yes.

"Hey, fucker, why don't you tell us why we're here?" Robert asked.

"Be easy on the man," she said to him.

"This guy just ruined our opportunity to get out of here," Robert said.

Darla shook her head. "And you'll have another chance tomorrow."

"You don't know that for sure."

Martin looked up at Robert, fear glazing his eyes. "Every night at 6:00 pm."

"6:00 pm?" Floyd asked.

Martin nodded his head up and down. "Yes, yes, yes, yes. 6:00 pm was the time. Six, six, six."

"It's 9:00 pm for us," Darla said. "You were in another house?"

Martin swung his head around, having a good look at the place. "9 is a 6 but up...side... down. This house, it looks just like ours," he said.

"And where is your house?" Jesse asked.

Martin shrugged. "I don't know. I don't know."

"This guy is full of it," Lawrence said.

"How could you say that?" Darla said, telling him off. "How many were you?"

Martin swallowed, taking a second to think. "Seven of us. One for each sin. One for each deadly sin." He sobbed, curling up and rocking back and forth. The others looked at one another, confused at what was said. Darla shifted over, wanting to comfort the man. As she rested her hand on his back, Martin panicked and drew himself to the opposite side of the couch, making eyes like daggers at Darla.

"You're all going to die. I'm going to die. Those things are killing us for our sins."

Darla, wanting to calm him, said in a soft voice, "Martin, please don't—"

"We're going to die!" he shouted, and the room fell silent.

Martin spun his head around, looking at all of them with his sobbing, red eyes. His crying suddenly stopped, turning into something of a nervous chuckle. "My name here is not Martin. In my past life I was Martin, I always only cared about myself, my looks, always keeping up with those Joneses," he said, continuing to giggle.

"Thanks for lettin' this nut in here," Robert said to Darla.

"Oh…I'm not crazy. No, no, no, no, nonononono."

Darla leaned in again calmly, this time not laying a hand on him. "Can you tell us what happened to you?"

Martin began to cry again. "You want to know? I'll tell you, but only if you really want to know."

"We do," Floyd said.

Martin, still rocking back and forth and holding his bloody arm pressed against his chest—in need of a new towel with the blood soaking through—turned and looked at all of them. "Before I tell you what happened to me. You want to know who put us here?"

The room nodded.

Martin smiled. "Satan himself. He's watching, and always listening."

"The… devil?" Darla asked, but Martin didn't respond right away. He sat and stared at the floor; the others stood quietly, looking at one another, waiting. Jesse glared out the window, staring into the dark woods. Just when Robert was about to speak, Martin continued.

"I woke up in this house with people I'd never met before, just like... just like you guys. I had no idea how I even got there. In the house I was in, I was the only guy. For days we tried to find a way out, but eventually, being kept trapped in this place got to us. So, I had to go—as well as two others. We wanted to escape the devil's house. This purgatory. We had to. But those things out there... What they can do..."

"So, you come from a house just like this? But only with all women?" Floyd asked.

Martin looked up at him and nodded. "All of us were there for a reason. Just like you all. I wasn't proud of what I did."

"What did ya do?" Lawrence asked.

Martin shook his head. "I don't want to speak about it. We all did things wrong; that's why the devil placed us here."

Robert took a step forward, giving a light chuckle in disbelief. "And what did we do, smart guy?"

Martin stared at the floor again. He then took a sip of his water, his left hand shaking as he did. As he brought the glass down, his eyes stayed looking at his feet. "We did terrible things, all of us, to the most innocent. You know what you did," Martin said, raising his head to the group. "Each of you knows what you did."

There was silence until Robert spoke up. "This guy is fucking bullshitting us. Just a part of this game and trying to spook us."

Martin chuckled, looking up at Robert, and he shook his head from side to side. "I'm not trying to scare you. I'm just telling you the truth."

Darla leaned in. "What do you know?"

"Fucker doesn't know anything!" Robert barked.

Darla turned to him. "Shut up," she said, bringing her attention back to Martin. "Please, tell us what happened."

His hand shook as he took another sip of water. Once he was done, he began his story.

"Our house cracked like an egg. I and two others—their names were Laura and Britney—seemed to be the only ones that had any sanity left. Kendra, she was Envy, she lost her fucking mind. You couldn't expect it either. She wore this red polka dot dress, her hair in a bun, and she was all thin and beautiful. She kind of looked like she had walked out of the '60s. She was saying and doing all sorts of weird shit."

"What was she saying?" asked Darla, leaning a little closer.

Martin paused. "How we were meant to die in here, and how this was going to be our home forever. She killed Sloth—cut her across the neck while she slept. Then she killed Greed, struck her with a blade in the back. So, Lust and Wrath and I—"

"You gave each other nicknames?" Lawrence asked.

Martin stopped and looked up at him with a disappointed look. "No, that's what we are here. Those are our true names now. All of us have done something horrible with a deadly sin."

"I didn't," Robert said.

"Let him continue," Darla said.

"Lust and Wrath... well, we wanted to leave the place. The previous day, we shaved down the tip of one of the stool legs, making a home-made spear, and we added it to the two knives we kept with us. The three of us decided that it was time to leave. We tried everything to get out, but there was no other way. None. So, we had to go. The next night, we went to gather food to take, not telling Envy that we were leaving. We'd take the food, and at 6:00 PM, we'd get out."

"Why didn't you kill Envy—whatever her name was?" Robert asked with suspicion.

"I'm no killer. I couldn't," Martin said.

"So, your nickname is Pride?" Lawrence asked with a laugh.

Martin looked up at him. "Again, no, that's my name here."

"Oh, hell. Okay. I'm just gonna stick to Martin."

Darla shook her head, then turned to Martin, "Go on, please."

Martin took his last sip of water, then put the glass on the couch. "As the three of us were leaving, we went to the kitchen to snag the food. There, Envy was already killing Gluttony—sticking her in the gut multiple times, blood splattering on her face with a gleeful smile. Gluttony dropped to the floor, her own mess pouring from her wounds. Envy told us it was because she was stealing. The three of us got out of there quickly, taking the food and heading out the door once it opened. The whole time Envy was just smiling, waving goodbye."

Martin stopped. He clenched his injured arm as he sat, and his gaze dropped back to his feet. The group, other than Robert, at least, remained glued to the story.

"We ran through those woods as fast as we could. I was hoping to God that nothing would happen. That those things out in the darkness didn't appear and come after us. We were hopeful. But, of course, the three of us were just being naive, I guess. It didn't take long for Britney to get it."

"Who's Britney?" asked Jesse.

"Sorry, Wrath," Martin responded, then he continued, "we heard them calling out our names. It scared the hell out of us, but we kept on running. Wrath got lost, though. Lust and I kept on going. I just ran and ran and ran. We heard Wrath's screams come shooting through those woods. We heard those things rip her apart. But we kept going. Give or take, we ran for a good half-hour or so until we heard strange noises."

"What kinda noises?" Lawrence asked.

Martin paused, his eyes to the floor still. "Like…waves. So, we—"

"Waves? What the fuck are you talking about?" Robert said, suddenly interested again.

Darla turned to him. "Do you ever shut your mouth?"

Robert stepped forward. "Are you honestly dumb enough to believe this fucker?"

"Look at his arm, Robert," Darla said. "You think he'd do that himself?"

Robert shook his head, stepping back and laughing.

Martin went on, "Yeah, we heard waves, and we followed the noise. As we did, it led us out of the woods, and we saw rocks and a huge drop down to a massive expanse of water. We're on an island."

"Oh, give me a fucking break," Robert said.

"Massive tidal water is coming in and out. If you were to climb down, it would take you close to an hour—that's in good daylight and if you were experienced. So that's what Laura, or Lust, and I did. I was the first to go down, climbing in the dark. It wasn't a good idea. We only had the starlight to guide us. Each step felt like it could have been my last. The wind from the sea kept swooshing in. I eventually made it to a rock that acted like a ledge—big enough for maybe three people. It had a rock above that acted like shelter too. As Laura came down, we heard the screams from those things. She hustled down too quickly in panic, took a misstep, screamed, then dropped, falling onto the rocks and waves below."

"Jesus Christ," Darla muttered.

Martin looked at her and nodded. "He's *not* on this island to help us."

"Was there some kind of dock or port you could make out?" Floyd asked.

Martin shook his head. "No, I didn't see anything like that. I slept there 'til morning. I woke up to a seagull squawking at me. I wanted to go down, that was the plan, but I remembered my spear was still up above. And, honestly, I didn't think I could climb down; I had no energy. I wanted to find something, you know, like a port as you said. So, I went back up, grabbed the spear, and walked the edge of the rocks as far as I could. Eventually, I had to stop. It felt like it wouldn't end. It just kept going and going, and I gave up around dusk."

"Did you see those things during the day at all?" Darla asked.

Martin shook his head. "No, I was scared of them. I kept my spear aimed as I walked, and I ate the little food that was left in the pillowcase we brought. My mind was cracking, though—dehydration and lack of food. I saw shit. I even thought that I was them sometimes. But then I realized it was my brain playing tricks. I ate the food that was left, but then I fell over and passed out. I woke up, and it was night. I started walking again, but then I heard those things calling out to me. So, I ran, but they caught up to me, and one attacked."

After he said this, Martin raised his arm. "But I was able to stick the little one with the spear. I ran for a little while longer, then, thankfully, I saw the light coming from your house and came running. And now, here I am." Martin looked at the group, then he gave a nervous smile.

"He's full of shit. And we shouldn't have let him in," Robert said, then he took off downstairs. The others stood in silence. Darla turned to Martin, giving him a comforting look. "Martin, you're telling us the truth, right?"

Martin nodded. "I'm not lying to you all. I'm not. I promise you. Guess he doesn't trust me?" he said.

Darla shook her head. "That's Robert, and nobody should trust him either."

Lawrence snorted, then asked his first question. "So, you don't know what's goin' on?"

Martin turned to him, staring and giving himself a moment to word his answer. "I feel that I may, but my answer couldn't possibly be 100% fact. It's been difficult…but I believe we are not in a familiar place."

"Well, ain't that obvious?" Lawrence responded.

"It is, yes. But I mean…well, what I'm trying to say is, this isn't Earth. At least, I don't think so."

"You said we are on an island?" Jesse asked.

"Yes, but—" Martin was interrupted as Robert came walking back into the living room, slowly taking a seat by the kitchen counter. Everyone turned to watch him arrive and sit. He didn't seem to want to be there, but maybe he felt as if he should. Martin then looked to continue once again.

Taking a breath, Darla could tell this was a lot for him. The man was traumatized. His hand shook—as did his leg—while he spoke. "I think we are at a place where it's made to look like we're on Earth, but we are not. At the house, it was similar to here; I'm going to guess. I'll say this, too. Each of us quickly realized that we had something that connected. That connection was one of the deadly sins. You know?"

"I can't remember all of them off the top of my head," Floyd admitted.

Darla thought for a moment. "Sloth, gluttony, envy…" She paused.

"Lust, pride, greed, and wrath," Floyd finished.

Martin nodded. "That's right. We found out we each connected to one. Those things out there"—Martin pointed to the window—"well, they're the devil's daughters, you see."

Robert chuckled. "Oh. My. God, you're nuts."

"I'm not," Martin said.

"Can't anyone be guilty of those crimes? What person hasn't felt lust or done something greedy, or... wrathful?" Floyd asked.

Martin paused, getting emotional. The others waited in silence until he continued. "All of us did something terrible to others under one of these sins. And now, God is punishing us. Punishing us for the bad that we have done." Martin paused. "Did you get the second envelope yet?"

"No," Floyd said, looking around.

"Oh, Jesus," Martin mumbled.

"What's it say?" Lawrence urged.

Martin looked up at them. "It's horrible. The other one. Did it just appear on the table?"

"Yes," Floyd confirmed.

"This one will too. The next one. That's if it's the same as ours. If you want flashlights in the darkness, someone must be blinded."

24

Night came, and the others went to sleep. Floyd took a shift to wait and watch for the envelope to appear as Martin had said. Their new guest lay asleep on the couch with his injured arm resting on his stomach. Floyd sat, waiting in the kitchen, his irritation growing from the mind-numbing silence and his blurry sight. The odd snore rose from Martin, which helped Floyd keep his eyes open. Sitting at the table, he played with his knife until he suddenly had the urge to go to the bathroom. He hadn't gone yet while here—possibly due to the stress and lack of water and food, but he went.

Taking only a moment away from the kitchen, Floyd tip-toed his way inside the bathroom, where he lifted the lid. The stench was putrid. "Jesus Christ," he muttered as he covered his mouth. Shaking his head, he just shut the lid and opted to take a piss down the tub drain. Once he was done, he zipped up his fly, did up his belt, and opened the door.

When he did, a dark figure walked past the hallway, heading down the stairs.

"Hey!" Floyd yelled.

The dark figure was already heading towards the door. Floyd moved as quickly as he could with his knife in his hand, but as soon as he cut the corner of the hallway, the figure—a dark-cloaked being with no face seen—stepped outside. Floyd ran down the steps, but the door shut, locking instantly. He tried the handle, but it was locked for good. Looking out the window, he saw whatever it was drift with eerie grace back into the woods. Floyd banged his fist against the window, furious that he had just missed him.

As he stepped away from the door, Floyd saw Jesse had woken and stepped out of the hallway. "What is it?" he asked Floyd. Leaping up to the top level, Floyd went right to the table. There he saw the envelope had been left. "Fuck," Floyd said.

Jesse was curious but mostly nervous. "Please, talk, man. What is it?"

Floyd then turned to Jesse, holding up the envelope. "I just missed him," he said with frustration.

"Who?

"The person who put this here."

"An intruder?" Jesse asked.

"What in the blue fuck is goin' on?" Lawrence asked as he stepped out of the hallway.

"We had a visitor, I guess," Jesse said, filling Lawrence in.

"I just saw a guy drop this off. Left the house; door was open. He shut it, and it locked, and he just took off casually into the woods."

"You didn't see no face?" Lawrence asked.

Floyd shook his head. "No, I didn't." Then, taking the envelope, Floyd opened it. The others were so focused on the situation that they didn't notice that they had woken up Martin.

His voice crept over as they spoke. "It will want you to go blind," he said. The others heard him and turned back around. None answered. They knew but had to open it anyway as Floyd unfolded the envelope with the happy face on it. With 'X's for eyes instead of dots this time. He took the paper out and revealed it.

It read:

> There is darkness in the woods, too much so to see,
> but take a house member's sight,
> and you will be given the gift of light.

The three in the kitchen glanced at the poem, reading it repeatedly, knowing what it meant, yet still needing time to digest it.

Martin stood and walked over to them, clasping his arm against his stomach—this time with the bloody towel loose around his arm, almost touching the floor. "I told you. I'm no liar," he said.

JESSE

"Daddy, I don't feel good today."

"I know, sweetheart."

"I just want the pain to go away."

Jesse sat brushing his daughter Ellie's hair back as she lay in bed. He smiled at her. "Sweetheart, the pain will be over one day."

"But when, Daddy?"

"I don't know, sweetheart."

Ellie began to cry as she curled up in bed, scrunching the sheets with her hands and pulling them closer. Her complexion was pale; she was in her pyjamas with a housecoat wrapped around her underneath the bed covers to combat the chills.

"Hey, you know that song Daddy wrote that I sent out online?"

Ellie nodded her head.

"It's had lots of listeners. So many that people are donating now since I had to quit my job for you." Jesse smiled, and so did Ellie. "Money is coming in, so Daddy doesn't have to work any longer. I'll be your full-time caretaker."

"I'm sorry, Daddy."

Jesse shook his head. "Sweetheart, don't be sorry. I'm so happy that I get to stay at home with you."

"Are people feeling bad for me?"

"Yes, but that's okay. People want you to get better, sweetheart," Jesse said, taking a glass of water and giving it to her. After she swallowed the water, Jesse placed the glass on the nightstand next to her.

"You're a little internet star now," Jesse said, smiling.

Ellie smiled. "What's wrong with me?"

Jesse shrugged. "Not sure, Ellie. Nobody knows yet."

"Well, why haven't I seen a doctor yet?"

Jesse brushed her head again. "Because doctors are ignorant. Daddy knows what's best for you."

"Would they hurt me, Daddy?"

He nodded his head. "Yes, but not intentionally. They'd think they'd be helping you. But they would only make things worse."

"I don't understand."

"I know, I know, it's okay. Don't worry, though. You'll feel better one day."

Ellie's stomach growled from underneath the sheets. Jesse heard the noise, and Ellie whined, curling up. He leaned over and kissed her on the forehead. Looking into her eyes, he gave her a comforting smile. "Chicken noodle?" he asked. Ellie nodded with her eyes shut, and Jesse left the room.

Opening the can of chicken noodle, it plopped into the sauce-pot. Filling the can with water, Jesse dumped it in and began to stir it while switching the element rise to a medium heat. A *ping* came from his laptop nearby. Jesse had a browse—another donation of $150 dollars added to the fund. That gave a total of $2000 of donations in just one week. A smile grew, and Jesse's heart felt warm. Then, taking out a white substance from under the sink which he had purchased on the street, Jesse poured a small amount of it in the pot as he stirred, mixing it in well.

25

The house had violence lingering in the air. Darla, Floyd, and Martin stayed upstairs, while Robert, Lawrence, and Jesse were with one another in the basement. Even with everyone in their clique, they still stayed an arm's length away, keeping an eye on each other so they could keep their own precious eyes. Nobody trusted anyone. Not. A. Soul.

Robert sat quietly, keeping to himself, as did Jesse and Lawrence. He had had a great idea while he was eating his breakfast—a piece of chicken and a slice of bread. He thought of those flashlights. What if he was able to obtain them? Robert was more than desperate to get the fuck out of this house—and having Martin as a new guest made him want to leave even sooner. Who the fuck was that guy and all this nonsense he spoke? He tried to go earlier, and now, he wanted those flashlights. Robert stood up, catching both Lawrence and Jesse's attention. Walking over to the bottom of the basement stairs, he kept an ear out for Darla and

Floyd, hearing them chatting in the living room. Robert wanted to pitch his idea and how all three were going to get out.

Making his way over to the couch that Jesse sat on, he made himself comfortable, whispering. "Listen," Robert said, and Lawrence and Jesse, a little nervous, leaned in to hear what Robert had to say. He took one last look over his shoulder before he pitched his idea. "We stay one more night. Tonight, I blind that Martin guy. I'll kill 'im too—won't let him suffer. Like the past gift of water, I take it we'll receive the flashlights tomorrow morning. Then, we take the food and peace on out of here." Robert gave a smile once he finished, hoping they'd agree.

Lawrence and Jesse turned to look at one another, then back at Robert. Still keeping their voices low, Jesse spoke first. "Did you not hear that guy say we were on an island? It's fucking useless, man."

Lawrence nodded. "I think that ain't goin' to be an option for us anymore, Robert."

Robert shook his head. "Listen, those things out there; those are not demons—no fucking way. We can kill them. Three grown men against a woman and her little girl."

"Those things out there are something else. You heard the loud cries they make," Jesse said.

"Whatever they are, guys, there are three of us and two of them. This Martin fellow, sure he may have seen water—

if he's even telling the truth—but maybe he only saw one side? What are our options anyways, fellas, huh? Die in this shithole, or give it our best go out there?"

"Oh, hell I-I don't know," Lawrence said.

Robert smiled. "You do, Lawrence, come on. Don't tell me Martin changed your mind now."

"I think I'll stay here," Jesse said.

"Jesse, you know you can't rot here. That's what's going to happen if we don't make some sort of attempt. How can you even sleep now at night with that stranger in the house?"

Jesse smiled. "I only met you the other day; what is the difference?"

Robert rested his hand on Jesse's shoulder. "We woke up at the same time."

"That doesn't mean anything. For all I know, you are a part of this," Jesse said, shrugging his shoulder away from Robert's hand.

Robert couldn't believe that Jesse would make such an assumption. Maybe it was the hunger, the desperation, or the cabin fever setting in, but Robert cared that Jesse said these words. His face went flush red. "How fuckin' dare you? I'm the one making plans to get us out of here, while you just want to sit around, waiting for help we sure as hell aren't going to get."

"Oh, you don't know that," Jesse said.

"Well shit. Fine. I say it may be dangerous right now, but hell, *maybe* I should go," Lawrence said, giving a nod to Robert. "I'm gonna starve in here anyway. What the hell's the difference? "

* * *

Darla had Martin's injured left arm held over the bathroom sink while Floyd stood behind, arms crossed and holding his knife. With a small amount of water at the bottom of a glass, Darla poured it over Martin's fresh wound. Barely any blood ran down his arm, and Martin winced as the cold water flushed out his wound a little. Once all the water was poured, Darla wrapped his arm with a fresh towel. "How's that?" she asked.

Martin looked at her, still with a little bit of scrunch in his face as the towel wrapped around, touching the raw, open skin.

In the living room, they took a seat on the couch. Martin lay his head back, and shutting his eyes, he said, "Thank you," to Darla softly.

She smiled. "Of course."

Floyd had a seat, stretching his legs out while rubbing his eyes. Darla sat beside him, resting her arm on his back. "How are you doing?" she asked. Floyd shrugged, clearly bothered. "I have sight you know—just with a tinge of a

blur. It's giving me a headache—that and the dehydration."
Darla felt for him, yet she had no words. She continued
rubbing his back for comfort as Floyd shut his eyes and
leaned forward, trying to get a grip on his throbbing head.

"Tell me about your family," Floyd said.

Darla smiled. "Well, my late husband, Evan, was a
dentist. We had been together since we were fourteen. Love
of my life. A wonderful father, an incredible husband. Last
year he was diagnosed with brain cancer." Darla took a
moment of pause. "It was a Tuesday—12pm on the nose—
when he passed. I was with him when he left us. I miss him
so much, and so do the kids. Olivia is my oldest. She's about
to head into middle school. Smart as a whip. Both my kids
are, but she loves school, whereas my son can't be bothered.
How typical." She chuckled.

"Olivia is a musical girl. She loves to draw and has
recently gotten on the soccer team at school. She's a handful.
My son, well, he's a little younger—still in grade school.
Loves recess so far, that's it. Gym class, too, I guess. Right
now, he's being picked on at school. That's the problem
right now. Just kids being kids. I'd want him to know that
he's not alone, that the bullying will end. I hate thinking
about it. My son will be wondering where I am right now.
Both of them—but especially Luke. He's so innocent."

Darla stopped talking. She found that Floyd had
become the one rubbing the other's back for comfort. He

smiled at her, and even though he couldn't see 20/20, Floyd could tell Darla had become misty-eyed thinking of her children.

'There, there," he said. "You'll see them again soon. Like I said earlier, it's a promise I'm making you."

Darla smiled, wiping away a tear. "This is all just so messed up," she said, giving a weeping giggle.

"It certainly is," Floyd agreed with a tone of reflection.

"Do you have children, Floyd? I'm sorry, I may have already asked this."

Floyd smiled. "It's okay, no. I don't. I just have my mother to care for."

He seemed pretty sombre when he said this, and Darla could sense something was up. She felt the urge to ask, so, re-framing the question, she said: "*Did...* you have children?"

Once the subject had left her lips, there was silence. Floyd—hands together, tapping his foot, staring at the floor, and taking in a breath—thought for a moment that felt precious. Turning to Darla, with sadness on his face, he said, "Yes, but she passed." Those words hit Darla in the gut.

"I-I'm so sorry," Darla said, almost trembling. Floyd rubbed her shoulder, giving her a soft smile that cut through his sadness. "You're going to see your children again and live a wonderful life with them. We will get out; you have my word."

26

Jesse slept with one eye open. He had to. He lacked sleep, but he couldn't rest due to the situation and what a conundrum it was. As he lay on his back, staring into the darkness, he began to think of his first-ever gig. It was easy for him to visualize. When you're losing your mind, the daydreams seem more real. He imagined his first gig at the local pub near his parents' place. He stepped up on stage, gear already set up for him. He began strumming his air guitar while in bed, keeping himself in the false reality. With a smile on his face, Jesse was back in his happy place until a knock on his door crumbled his vision.

Jesse sat up, his eyes darting towards the door as he pushed himself to the other side of the bed.

"Who's there?' he said.

The door slowly opened, revealing the silhouette of Robert. "It's me," Robert whispered.

Jesse frowned, dropping his bushy eyebrows. He recognized that voice. "What do you want?" he asked, grazing his hand around the sheets near him, hoping to find where he put his knife. Robert stepped in, and as he did, Jesse leaned a little farther away, all his muscles tensed. Robert, with both hands raised, revealed he had no weapon, letting Jesse know he came in peace.

"Please, come with us tomorrow," Robert said.

Jesse shook his head. "No way. No fucking way."

Robert moved with caution as he sat on the bed. At this time, Jesse had found his knife in the darkness. He didn't raise it, but he did grasp the handle.

"Please, Jesse, hear me out," Robert said, keeping his voice down to a whisper. Jesse stared, not saying anything in response. There was a pause in the room, and Jesse shrugged, wanting Robert to get it over with and speak.

"We go out tomorrow, right. We have weapons made—Lawrence is already working on one. We'll take all the food, water, and head out. But listen. Those things out there won't have a chance. They're already injured if Martin stabbed one. That means we can kill them."

"That does not mean we can kill them," Jesse responded, keeping his voice low.

"Well, at least we can hurt them, slow them down. And, hear me out, that Lawrence guy... well, he's not to be trusted," Robert said, leaning in even closer as he spoke.

"Nobody here is."

"Nah, he's got plans, man. He wants to leave, but if we fail, he told me that he wants to eat us. Not me, but you, Martin, Floyd, and Darla."

"Wait. What?"

"He wants to attempt to leave. But say, we fail, and we have to head back, he will start to kill everyone and eat them. Guy's next fucking move is cannibalism."

"Are you bullshitting me?"

"No, so I need you tomorrow. I need you. The three of us, out there, helps our chances, and not only that, once we face those things, if they do start to overpower us, the two of us, Jesse, have only got to be faster than that fat fuck Lawrence. He'll fall behind, and he's got enough meat on him to give them hours of feasting. Leaving us two with the chance to get away."

Jesse hesitated. "I don't know."

"I'll do the dirty work, alright, Jesse. Tonight, I plan on blinding Martin—he'll fight back the least. Plus, I wanna' fucking rub it in Darla and Floyd's face, us leaving with most, if not all, of the food and water. I blind our new guest, we get our flashlights, and then we take off. What do you say?" Jesse couldn't see it, but Robert gave an enthusiastic smile.

"Well, first, I think you're fucking crazy. Second, the letter said a house member has to go blind if we want flashlights. Martin, though he's here now, may not count.

Think about it; he's really just a guest, not an original member of this house. So, that might not work. If you want me to go, blind someone like Darla. I know you want her to suffer in here, you misogynistic pig. But if you want to let her see you smile as you escape, go for Floyd. Even Floyd—he's almost blind now due to you crunching his glasses. If you do him in, I'll go with you."

There was a moment of silence.

Robert sat, taking in what Jesse had just said. "Do you not trust me?" Robert asked, concerned. "Out of everyone here, do you honestly not?"

Jesse regretted saying so much, but he'd blame it on stir crazy after this conversation. "Look, Robert, we all know you're capable of killing. I know you'd be able to blind someone as well."

"I-I didn't kill Ken," Robert interjected with frustration in his tone.

Jesse smiled. Even in the darkness, Robert was a lousy liar. "Sure, Robert, sure."

"Fuck you," Robert said, restraining his anger.

Still whispering, Jesse said, "No, Robert, just listen to what I have to say. Blind Darla or Floyd, and I'll join you. I know how desperately you'd love for them to see you leave, but just do it. If you don't, I'll let Lawrence know about you wanting him to be tomorrow's main course." Jesse lifted his knife towards him, and though the bleeding kitchen light's glow from the open door subtly lit the room, Robert still couldn't see it.

Jesse smiled; this Robert could see." Do the smart thing, will you?"

Robert clenched his fists again. "*That bushy eyed fuck,*" he thought.

Robert stood from the bed, giving Jesse a nod. Taking in a deep breath, he exhaled to calm his frustration. Smiling, and still whispering, Robert gave his final words for the night, "I hate you, Jesse, I do. For many reasons. But right now, I hate you because you're right. I'll do in Floyd because, more than ever, I'd love to give Darla that wink and smile goodbye."

Jesse, his knife still pointing in Robert's direction, whispered, "Good luck. We'll get out tomorrow and get on our way home."

Robert didn't say anything. Approaching the door, he stepped out, shutting it behind him. Jesse heard his footsteps take off down the hallway. He exhaled with relief, lowered his knife, and lay back down, resting his head on the pillow. He kept the blade in his grip. Within a few minutes, Jesse was able to fall half-asleep at best.

Hours passed that only felt like seconds, but then Jesse sat up as a clattering noise was heard in his room. His breath gained weight, heavy and slow. "Who's there?"

Silence.

"Robert?" he asked, trembling, but the room was dark and quiet. It was paranoia, he figured, getting the best of him.

27

Resting his head on his pillow, Jesse exhaled and made himself comfortable. His hand still gripping the blade, he smiled, shutting his eyes. He was thinking of his first gig once again. The good times, the drinks, and the music. The first place he planned on visiting once he escaped this house with the three of them together. Him, Robert, and Lawrence taking on those creatures—there wouldn't be a problem. And if they were on a rock, there had to have been a dock for a boat, somewhere.

WHAM!

It felt like a giant stone had dropped on his face. His nose was shattered. The sudden shock and pain from the blow caught his breath. Mouth wide open, he felt a hand covering it and pushing down, pressing against his teeth. Before he tried to scream, Jesse's first reaction was to grab hold of his assailant's wrist, which he did. Then, opening his eyes, he could only make out the shape of the arms. He let out his first muffled scream, but it cut short from the knife's blade that drove through his throat. The pain was sudden and excruciating. The knife's blade then left his jugular, and when it did, Jesse's eyes went wide.

The sight from his left eye instantly vanished as the tip of the bloody blade punctured through his pupil like a bullseye, caving it in, bursting the eyeball like an egg half-poached. Jesse tried to scream, but the wound from his throat wouldn't allow it. Blood chugged upwards like a volcano erupting. He thrashed his arms and kicked his legs, but it was no use. The attacker struggled to keep Jesse under control. Gripping his head the best he could, keeping him still, the blade bombed down again. It missed the eye and stuck Jesse only half an inch underneath, still puncturing through soft tissue. The knife came again. The attacker didn't miss the second time, bursting the right eye clean through. Blood, eye juice, and tears ran down his cheeks.

Jesse, blind and with a punctured throat, felt the attacker let go. His ears, still working well, heard a whispering voice, "Should have trusted me."

Robert smiled, then he turned and left the bedroom, closing the door behind him.

Jesse held onto his throat with his left hand, and rolling over to his side, he swung his right out ahead above the bed. Pushing himself off, Jesse dropped and hit the floor with a thud. Still kicking his legs, and thrashing his free arm, Jesse splayed. In a panic for help, he got to his knees, bumping himself against the bedroom door. His life was now in forever darkness—depending on if he lived at all.

With desperate speed, his bloody right hand felt the knob of his door. The blood from his palms kept himself from getting a good grip. He tried to scream again but wasn't capable. Finally, he got enough hold to open the door, blood rushing out of his throat, spilling down his green sweater and jeans, onto the floor. Pulling the door open just enough to slip through, Jesse got on all fours, crawling towards the living room.

Martin heard the commotion first. He was already up, having been busy in the bathroom. He stepped out and ran up behind Jesse, who kept crawling before dropping to the floor like a sack of stones. Floyd, dozing off already, stood to attention with the sound. Opening the door to Room 2, he saw Jesse, eyes punctured and still breathing. With every breath he took in, more blood rushed out. Floyd saw Martin standing behind Jesse, back in shock mode from the bloody scene. The sight of Jesse made Floyd begin to retch. He'd seen some fucked up shit so far, but now, it was all too sudden. As Floyd threw up, only water seemed to come out with little chunks of bread mixed in.

Robert waited, listening in his room. Slipping on his black jacket again, he zipped it up this time, hiding his now-bloody shirt. Robert was in Room 3, which meant he could step out just behind them. As he did, he stood and pretended to be in horror of the scene. "What the fuck!" he cried out. Martin spun around, locking eyes with Robert. Taking a step back, Robert glared at Martin up and down. "You did this, didn't you, stranger?"

Instantly, in a pleading kind of way, Martin shook his head no. Floyd glared at him after he threw up what he could muster and watched as Martin span his eyes to him and Robert, desperately shaking his head.

"You did, you fucking killer," Robert said.

Darla stepped out, and as she was about to speak, the words stuck In her throat. The scene of the crime took her breath away as Martin stood guiltily above Jesse's body. Robert stepped out in the hallway. "He stuck him with Jesse's knife!" he said, shock in his voice.

'I-I didn't. R-really, I-I couldn't—"

"But you did," Robert said, "You were the one who knew about the next envelope. You had a plan."

"N-no. I—"

"You killed him; you killed him. You fucking killed him!"

Robert then drove his fist across Martin's face, knocking Martin against the wall. He slid to the floor, and his head slumped down to his chest and landed next to Jesse's waist in the puddle of blood left by his throat. Darla wanted to do something, but she just couldn't. It was all sudden; it was all too much.

Robert turned to Floyd, then to Darla, "You two, you both planned this, didn't you—with Martin. You're all killers, all of you. All of you!"

Floyd shook his head, holding his stomach as he stood. "We didn't do this, Robert. We didn't."

FLOYD

It was 11 pm, and Floyd sat in his car in the casino parking lot. He'd had no luck tonight. The night began with $600 in his wallet in bills, and now he was cleaned out. Nothing left to even fill up for a tank of gas tonight, adding another addition to his credit card. Reaching over to his glove box, he opened it and fished out a pack of cigarettes he'd hidden behind all the junk. His hands shook from stress, frustration, and self-pity. It had been two months since he'd had a smoke. The last time he did, he lost a hell of a lot more at this very casino. Slipping a cig out of the packet, Floyd lit it with the lighter in his car and got out, not wanting Tiffany to smell what he had done in the car.

With his hands still shaking, Floyd slipped the packet of smokes into his blazer, then took the first drag, letting the smoke trickle in, feeling the goodness it gave. While he leaned on the door of his car, Floyd exhaled the smoke and watched the casino lights flicker and blare its alluring colours, pulling in the suckers and gambling addicts like him to blow everything away. Taking off his glasses, Floyd pinched the bridge of his nose with his free hand, took a deep breath, and then rubbed his eyes.

"*You're nothing but a weak fool. Always unable to keep your word to yourself and anybody,*" he thought.

With his attention kept on his inner voice and sight on the casino that robbed him, a voice broke out. "Hey, bro!" the voice said. Floyd brought his attention to his right.

There, a man in his late fifties, tall with long hair and dressed in a suit with a tie undone, came out of the darkness towards him. Putting on his glasses, he had a better look at the fella. As he took the smoke out of his mouth, Floyd asked, "Can I help you?"

"Rough night?" the man said.

"Only when I choose to come to visit this place," Floyd said, sticking the smoke back in his mouth and taking another drag from the cigarette. Floyd caught the smoke the wrong way and began a coughing fit to end all coughing fits.

The stranger broke out in a drenched whiskey laugh. "Not much of a smoker, are you?" he asked. But Floyd kept coughing, shaking his head no.

The man smiled. "Must have had a real bad one tonight."

Floyd gathered himself then said, "Bad, sure, but not my worst night in losses. So, if 'you're planning on robbing me, that place there"—Floyd pointed to the casino ahead of him with the cigarette in hand—"got to me first, so I've got nothing for you."

The stranger leaned against the car, hands now slipping into his pocket. "Nah, friend, I'm here to bum a smoke off ya." Floyd turned to the man who made himself quite comfortable beside him, gave himself a moment to ponder, then reached into his blazer to grab the pack. Floyd stopped with the cigarette still in the corner of his mouth, keeping his hand in his blazer, turning to the man to his right. "Tell me a joke," Floyd said.

"A joke?" replied the man.

"Yeah, a joke. It's been a bitch of a night, and I wanna hear a joke. My actions tonight have just added to my money problems once again. I broke a promise to my girlfriend and will disappoint my sick mother. So, if you want a cigarette, tell me a joke to cheer me up."

The stranger smiled, nodded, and brought his attention to the casino lights, thinking of what to say. "A man walks into a bar, orders 15 shots of bourbon, and starts drinking them down as fast as he can. The bartender asks, 'hey, mister, why are you drinking so fast?' The man replies, 'You would be drinking fast if you had what I had.' The bartender looks at him, confused, 'Well, what do you have?' The guy looks up at him, '1 buck.' There, how's that?" the man asked with a chuckle.

Floyd laughed, "Sure. Alright, here you go." He took out the pack and slipped out a smoke for the man. He lit the end of the stranger's cigarette with the end of his. The man took a drag. "You got a problem then, with gambling?" he asked.

Floyd nodded. "Huge. I've been a good boy lately. But not tonight."

"Why tonight?" the man asked, taking a puff.

"I don't know. Hell, I don't know what's wrong with me. I'm in so much damn debt; it's

sickening. I've got responsibilities, bills to pay, and a mother to take care of, and here I am, throwing away my money on this bullshit," Floyd said, dipping his head down, now glaring at his feet.

"I'll tell you another one," the man said.

Floyd looked up at him, smiled, and said, "Better be good."

"How many Irishmen does it take to screw in a lightbulb?"

Floyd smiled as he finished his cigarette, flicking the butt on the ground and crushing it

underneath his shoe. "How many?" he asked.

The man leaned in a little closer and smiled. "One. He holds it in while the room spins for him." The man then burst out laughing. Floyd shook his head and chuckled.

* * *

Floyd arrived home to tell Tiffany the news. But when he did, she stood up from her chair with a gleaming smile, wrapped her arms around him, and kissed him. This was the opposite reaction to what he was expecting given that he had arrived at midnight, still reeking of smoke. But, once her lips left his, he saw her gleaming smile. "Floyd, I have news," Tiffany said.

Floyd's heart raced. "What is it?"

"I'm pregnant," Tiff said, kissing him again.

Floyd's face went blank. He was just able to keep his smile arched from the great news. A baby would mean this new job he had recently gotten was practically useless. A baby would mean he'd be still swimming in his gambling debt and only keeping his head above water for the next ten years. She saw him, his face, not showing what she'd expected.

"What's wrong? Aren't you happy?" Tiffany asked, feeling something wasn't right with him.

Almost in a daze, Floyd looked at her and brought her a strange glare. "Are you going to keep it?"

Tiff let go of him and took a step back. The question crushed her joy. "Am I? Yes, I am."

"That's a hell of a lot of money. A baby. We're already up to our eyeballs in debt," Floyd said.

"But, Floyd, we will make it work."

"No, we won't."

"But, Floyd."

"Tiffany, it's got to go. You have to get rid of it. Money is not what we have. It's unfair to the baby, and it's unfair on us."

"It's unfair on us? Or you, Floyd?"

"I finally gotta better paying job, Tiff. I finally can rid myself of the debt that I have."

She stepped closer, trying to calm her nerves, resting her hand on his shoulder. "Please, Floyd, you can still rid yourself of the debt. Of course, it'll just take a little longer with a child."

Floyd took a moment to ponder. Shaking his head, he looked at Tiff with sorrow in his eyes. "No, I'm sorry, with my mother being sick and you being off work, all I make will go to taking care of my mother, you, and that child. It can't happen. You have to get rid of it."

Tiffany slapped Floyd across the face, and the room fell silent. Floyd turned and brought his eyes in shame to hers. Shaking her head, Tiffany took a step back with her arms crossed, disgusted. "We want kids, Floyd; we've spoken about this. This is our baby. And it's my body. I'm keeping it.

We will make this work."

* * *

Floyd lay in bed, staring into the darkness. His thoughts were running wild. His feelings strongly told him that Tiffany was in over her head. She hadn't a clue what she was thinking—overjoyed by the news. Her thinking wasn't clear. Floyd knew it wasn't going to work. He was angry. She wasn't thinking about his needs. Until the kid would be off to school, and Tiffany was back to work… but then his sick mother, Karen, needed his assistance until the day she died. Floyd knew he had to do something. Or should he?

* * *

Seven months passed, and Floyd's debt only grew as they prepared for the child. Floyd and Tiffany sat at the kitchen table. She wouldn't stop telling the world about their exciting news, but Floyd hadn't told a soul in that time. Before Tiffany dropped the bomb on him about the pregnancy, Floyd felt the world lift off his shoulders slightly.

When he received his first paycheck in his new position, it was more money than he'd ever had in his life. He had doubts about his plans in life, almost discarding them. But when that paycheck came in, it all came back. He knew he wasn't a bad person. Floyd just had to do something ugly and necessary for everyone. But deep down, he knew, no matter what he told himself to sleep well, he would rid the baby from the world or for himself.

Tiffany drank tea with her tuna sandwich, crunching into the toasted baguette that Floyd had made for her. He could tell she was enjoying it as she crunched down, sipping her tea. Floyd kept up a smile as Tiffany rambled on about cribs she saw for sale. Floyd just sat and listened as she drank her tea—tea that he'd spiked. He knew she'd get sick, but whatever the name of the stuff he'd put in her drink was called, he felt strongly that Tiff wouldn't be harmed. That was until later that night, when she called out his name in panic.

When Tiffany called for him, Floyd thought it could have been Tiffany finding his mother dead in bed. But it wasn't. She was slumped over the chair in the living room as he ran over—retching, trying to throw up. He patted her back, held onto her arm, and brought her to the bathroom toilet. Tiffany hung her head over the bowl, trying desperately to throw up.

"What's goin' on?" Floyd's mother asked as she stood by the doorway.

"Call the doctor," Tiffany begged.

Floyd pattered her back, terrified and remorseful for what he had done. "It'll be fine, Tiff, just relax."

"I'll go," Floyd's mother said as she wobbled to the kitchen phone.

"Don't!" Floyd burst, glaring with almost deadly eyes at his mother. She was taken back, as was Tiffany, as she looked up at him from her head around the bowl. Tiffany frowned, confused at his reaction. Floyd turned back, staring at her and pushing his glasses back to the bridge of his nose. He was petrified over what he'd done. For the past two weeks, he hadn't wanted to do it. He had changed his mind around the terrible thoughts of ridding her of the baby. But when those paychecks kept coming in, Floyd changed his mind on a whim. Tiffany, looking at her boyfriend, the man she thought she knew, saw in his eyes his guilt, using all his emotional willpower to push through it.

28

They flipped Jesse over. His body was drenched in blood, and he lay on the floor, his back, arms and legs spread. Darla and Floyd were the only ones in the hallway, with Martin now in shock and out on the couch and Robert back downstairs with Lawrence. Floyd held onto Jesse's wrists while Darla had his ankles. They lifted together on the count of three and carried the man to Room 2. Ken had been shoved to the other side to make room for Jesse's corpse. Lifting Jesse inside, they brought his body onto the bed, resting him on his back next to Ken. Floyd took Jesse's hands and brought them together on his chest.

29

"Why'd you do it?" Robert asked. He was back upstairs with Lawrence beside him in the kitchen. Floyd and Darla stood in the living room, with Martin behind them, now sitting up on the couch. Darla scoffed at Robert's question but didn't answer.

Robert, with his arms crossed, frowned at her. "Something funny?" he asked.

Darla lifted her head, shaking it like a disappointed parent. "Oh, Robert, you're such a fool," she said to him, smiling after.

Robert took a couple of steps towards her, almost stepping out of the kitchen before leaning against the fridge. "Oh?"

"Yeah, this whole time, Floyd and I have been against killing anyone here. Now you think we'd both have the guts to blind someone, then kill them?" she said.

Lawrence spoke up. "That's just what you want us thinkin'."

Robert kept his eyes on Darla yet spoke to Lawrence. "What do you say, Lawrence? Once we get those lights, we should head on out of here."

Martin stood up, interjecting before Lawrence had time to speak. "You'll die out there, with those things."

Robert smiled at Martin. "Your story was bullshit. Those things can be killed. Lawrence and I can take them. And we will. Then, when we do, we'll both find a way out of here."

Martin stepped forward. "You can't leave. Those things—"

"Shut the fuck up," spouted Lawrence.

Robert pointed his finger at Martin. "You only saw one side of this place. If you think we're on an island, then there has to be a way for us to get off. Unless this is the coastline, and then we just go and find someone who will help us or die trying."

Martin sat back down, rocking himself back and forth, sobbing. He spoke to himself, staring blankly towards the floor. "Door opens we die, door opens we die, door opens we die, door opens we die, door opens we die, door opens we die, door opens we die, door opens we die... We're all going to die. Jesus, we're all going to die, we're all going to die."

"Shut up! We're getting out of here tomorrow at 9:00 pm. We will be gone, taking a body that *you* killed and using it as bait. Lawrence and I will be taking a ration of food before we go. Water as well. No discussion," Robert said, then stormed off. Lawrence gave both Darla and Floyd a nod before heading downstairs.

30

It was early morning. Robert and Lawrence had decided to stay downstairs while Floyd and Darla slept in Room 5. Martin had fallen asleep on the couch in the living room. The night was quiet, even peaceful. Martin had the best sleep he'd had since his arrival in this world. His body seemed to need it. Even with all the stress and hunger pains, Martin had passed right out. That was until 3:26 am when things started to feel weird.

He rose from the couch, trembling. His breathing was heavy, and his heart was beating like a son of a bitch. Such deep thuds that it hurt. Martin's mind felt like it was spiralling—as if he had vertigo. Holding onto the arm of the couch, he tried to ground himself, breathing in slowly, giving him a strange tingling sensation. The light from the kitchen still gave off a strong glow. So, unwrapping his arm, Martin had a look at his wound. Once the towel opened up, he almost tossed up his insides.

The wound was nightmarishly grotesque. His arm was turning gray. Where there would normally be blood, it seemed more like black goo, and the already torn skin was covered in puss at the edges. A strange, bumpy rash had developed that was so red and irritated it made him want to itch it just looking at it. Looking closer at his arm, Martin saw his veins closest to the wound were darkening and clogging with whatever that black goo was that he was now producing.

Martin panicked, tears shedding, shaking his head, and begging to be okay. His stomach churned—not from what he just saw, but from something else. Getting up, Martin left his towel behind, making his way to the bathroom. As he went inside, he closed the door quietly but quickly. Lifting the lid of the toilet, the horrid smell of the piled shit from the past few days flew up under his nostrils. It smelt horrible, but he didn't have time to care. Martin dumped his insides into the toilet. He kept his eyes shut the entire time; Martin chucked up what felt like half of his body weight.

After he was done, Martin felt relieved, and he slid, exhausted, to the floor. Cold sweat dripped down his face, running across his cheeks. At least, the floor felt cold, which was a relief. After ten minutes of lying on the floor, he stood up, weak and hunched over. When he did, he suddenly felt something loose in his mouth. Going to the mirror, he tried to see what it was. But there wasn't enough light from the window above. Opening the door, Martin let the kitchen light into the room. The glow was dim, but it was enough for him to see by. Whatever it was, he caught it and spat it out in the sink. In the pile of his bloody saliva, sliding slowly towards the drain, was his back molar. Pinching it with his fingers, Martin looked at it in his palm.

Tossing it, it clattered and made its way down the little dark hole. Martin dug his dirty fingers into his mouth, trying to feel which back molar he had lost. While back there, he felt something he thought was the empty pit—like another tooth was pushing through. This bone, still premature, was sharp. Martin's mind was racing, and while looking at himself in the mirror, he saw terror on his face.

While he pulled his fingers out, he felt something else strange. Another loose tooth, on the other side—this time near the front. His canine tooth, he felt, was hardly staying in. With only a gentle tug, the tooth popped right out and dropped into the sink. Looking back up, blood trickled down his mouth from the open wound. It was mixed in with Martin's tears. Having a closer look, he again felt a premature, yet sharper tooth coming through his gum.

Stepping back, he shook, terrified. His body was falling apart right in front of him. His rash itched, and he couldn't resist scratching it, but as he did, his arm flared up with a fiery burning sensation. The rash stung, and Martin pulled his hand away, closer to his eyes, and that's when he saw it.

On the fingers that he had scratched with, Martin's fingernails lifted and came loose. It was unbelievable; he could hardly look. But Martin, with the thumb of his right hand, peeled away each fingernail with great ease, dropping them into the sink.

He wanted to throw up again. Dunking his head back over the shit-piled toilet, Martin, again, chucked up black gooey liquid. He hadn't noticed at first, but the second time, moving his head back and giving a touch more light to the bowl of the toilet, he saw what looked like tar flooding over all of the housemates' droppings. Martin pushed himself back, feeling weak, and he curled into a ball on the floor.

31

Morning came, and Floyd brought Darla some cheese and pork from the fridge with a glass of water for breakfast. Making themselves comfortable, Floyd handed Darla some cheese to start. Chowing down, Darla shut her eyes. The food was tasting better the longer they stayed there. Floyd sipped water. Darla finished first. When she did, she asked, "We should leave, after they do."

Floyd turned to her. "I don't disagree. I'm terrified to leave, but I'm also terrified of sitting here and rotting."

"Going with them tonight would be suicide. They'll feed us to the lions, no question about it."

"True," Floyd said, "but if we left the day after, and we used another body as bait—as they plan to tonight—it could work. Though, like them, we'd have to try the opposite way Martin went. He isn't well, though. I just saw him on the couch. He seems to be getting a fever."

"Infected wound, no doubt."

Darla lay back down on their bed, resting her head on the pillow. There was a moment of silence, then she spoke. "When I was younger, my father always read me poetry. There was one poet, in particular, and his name was Robert Frost. Have you heard of him?"

Floyd shook his head no.

"He's great. He went through so much tragedy in his life. The guy was plagued with grief. Yet, he kept writing. His parents died while he was young, he had to admit his sister into a mental hospital—where she eventually died—and he had three children who died, one of disease and two who ended their own lives. After all that, his wife died of heart problems."

Floyd took a breath. "My God."

"Yeah, awful. My father loved him. He learnt about him when he went back to school. He would always tell me his story and recite his favourite poem to me. When I think of him, I tell myself that, no matter how tough times get, I need to just keep on going. Corny, I know."

Floyd shook his head. "No, not at all. What's your favourite of his?"

Darla smiled. "This is the one my father always told me—it's called Stopping by the Woods on a Snowy Evening." Darla sat up from the bed, cleared her throat, then began.

"Whose woods these are I think I know.
His house is in the village though;
He will not see me stopping here
To watch his woods fill up with snow.

My little horse must think it queer
To stop without a farmhouse near
Between the woods and frozen lake
The darkest evening of the year.

He gives his harness bells a shake
To ask if there is some mistake.
The only other sound's the sweep
Of easy winds and downy flake.

The woods are lovely dark and deep.
But I have promises to keep,
And miles to go before I sleep,
And miles to go before I sleep."

"It's nice. I like it," Floyd said with a gentle smile.

"He would say it to me when I felt like the world was on my shoulders. Anytime I was in need of being uplifted." Darla paused for a moment before she spoke again, gazing at the wall in front of her. Emotion rinsed her words as she spoke to Floyd again. "My fondest memory of my father was when we first came to Canada. I remember helping him take out the trash. It was a cold, fall morning, which chilled us to the bone. As we walked out with the garbage to the end of our new home's driveway, it suddenly began to snow. I thought it was beautiful as it was a first and a surprise to us both. Then, when my eyes caught my father, I watched as he held his head up high, staring at the sky, letting each snowflake touch his skin. He had tears of joy. I've never seen a man so proud. My mother, Nadia, passed at childbirth, so he raised me by himself. His name was Daniel. He was a single father. A hard worker. A great man."

"I'm sure he was," Floyd said with a smile.

Darla turned to Floyd, her face somber and still. "When I was ten years old, Floyd, something terrible happened." Darla took a moment to collect her words. Tears began to form, but she held them back to start again. "My father stopped to get gas. I remember him filling the tank, then heading into the store to pay. I watched as he stood at the counter as another man came to rob the place. I heard the shouting and watched as my father step towards the man to try and stop him. Then I heard the sound, a loud *pop*. It was a gunshot. It was so loud I felt it in my chest. The robber took off running, and my father stumbled out of the gas bar, holding his bleeding stomach and dropping to the sidewalk outside."

"Jesus," Floyd said, turning away, exhaling a breath.

"I was terrified, but I got out and walked over to him. It's odd, the things you remember. When I went up to him, there was blood all over. I remember him looking away, then turning to me. He gave me a somber smile." Darla paused, muscling up the strength to speak. "His hand reached out to touch mine. I held onto him. His grip was weak and his palm was so cold and wet from the blood and snow."

Floyd watched as Darla began to cry. Moving himself closer, Floyd raised his hand and began to rub her back, comforting Darla as best he could. Wiping away her tears, she continued. "I felt it when he passed. His soul leaving his body." Darla wiped away more tears as she continued, "It wasn't fair what happened to him. He was a man who deserved better. To be with his daughter. I should have had him in my life. But I didn't. And now, here I am, not with my children. Not there for them. I will get out of this place, Floyd; I have to for Luke and Olivia. To be with them again, to see them grow, to give them all my love as long as I live. I have promises to keep, Floyd, and miles to go before I sleep."

32

Robert had Jesse by the wrists, dragging him down to the midsection of the house while Lawrence stuffed a pillowcase full of food from the fridge. Robert, pulling Jesse's body down the steps, laid his body out on the floor. A blood trail ran from Room 2 all the way down to the middle section. After he dropped the body, he glared out the window. The flashlights were left on the porch for them.

Darla and Floyd, after taking turns sleeping, came out of the bedroom. From there they followed the blood trail out to the living room and saw Lawrence stuffing the pillowcase, tying up the end. "Hey, how much are you taking?" Floyd said, demanding an answer.

"Fuck you," Lawrence said.

"Nah, not fuck me. How much are you taking?"

Lawrence placed the bag on the counter, then grabbed his knife, turning to Floyd as an attempt to intimidate him. He smirked, looking at him. "Blind boy, think you can stop me?" Darla took a step forward. "You don't need that much," she said, and Lawrence aimed the blade towards her.

"You don't think. Come stop us," Lawrence said, seeming more confident than ever. Robert stepped up behind Darla and Floyd, staying still on the steps.

"That's what we're taking. There will be some for you. But not much." Robert then winked at them both. "You can always eat Kenny-boy."

"Fuck you both. We won't let this happen," Floyd said.

"Step aside," Lawrence said. He had the pillowcase of food now thrown over his shoulder, and the knife was held in the same hand that was holding the pillowcase end. He then grabbed the home-made spear off the counter and held it in the other hand, aiming it at Floyd and Darla. Both of them had their knives, with Darla pointing hers at Robert, while Floyd had his aimed at Lawrence. Robert and Lawrence, at opposite ends, kept a smile on their faces.

"This is going to be a stand-off, is it?" Robert said, staring at Darla with a piercing glare.

"It doesn't have to be," Darla said.

"Then let Lawrence through."

"Not until you leave half the bag's worth of food on that counter."

"Fuck you, and keep dream'n'," Robert said.

"Be a good little pair ah kids and step on outta the way," Lawrence said, taking an easy, half-step forward.

In silence, Floyd gripped the handle of the knife. Violence felt like it was going to erupt at any second. The silence was deadly as the four all glared at one another, hoping that one on each side of the law here would crack. But all of them stayed put, waiting, staring.

TICK. TICK. TICK. TICK. TICK. TICK. TICK.

"Be smart. Move," Robert demanded.

"Leave more food," Darla ordered.

TICK. TICK. TICK. TICK. TICK.

The lock slid north. It was sudden, and it caught everyone's attention, breaking the tension for a moment, but it also turned out to be the trigger. As Floyd turned to the noise, Lawrence took his opportunity. With the back end of his spear, Lawrence swung the end of the stool leg and swatted Floyd across the face. His head whipped back, knocking him against the wall, and he slid to the floor. Lawrence then charged forward, and Darla turned towards him. As she did, Robert grabbed her from behind and shoved her across the couch, her top half folding over the edge.

Robert and Lawrence were in the middle section by the window beside the door. Looking outside the house, they saw no sign of the mother and daughter.

Martin awoke as he saw Darla shoved to the couch. He got up and saw her pushing herself up off the couch while the door opened. He immediately understood the situation. "You can't go out there!" he yelled.

The red door was open, and Lawrence and Robert were already outside, with Robert dragging Jesse's corpse out the door and off the porch onto the dirty grass, then coming back up and grabbing both flashlights. Darla stepped outside, shoving herself into Lawrence's back. He toppled over, tripping over Jesse's feet. As he landed, his spear tumbled to the ground, and Darla picked it up, aiming it at the two men. Robert saw Lawrence on the ground and Darla with the spear, and he grabbed his knife, pointing it at Darla.

"Are you fucking stupid?" Robert said before stepping over to Lawrence, snagging the pillowcase of food from the ground. Lawrence was taking ages to get back to his feet.

"Fuckin' bitch," he mumbled.

Sticking the end of the spear at the back of Lawrence's neck, but not puncturing him, held Lawrence still.

"Now, Darla, don't be doin' this," Lawrence begged as he stayed on all fours.

"Give us the food back. Give it back!"

Martin ran out of the doorway in a panic, and he didn't hesitate in grabbing Robert's arm. As he did so, Robert swatted Martin away, furious at his attempt to get hold of him.

"Get the fuck off me, man! Get off me!" Robert demanded, raging.

Martin, towel undone and laying on the ground, latched on and pulled at Robert, trying all he could to drag the man inside.

"You'll die!" Martin cried.

While Martin held Robert, Darla went for the pillowcase. Before she could, Robert stuck Martin in the opposite arm with the knife.

Martin let out a cry and dropped to the ground, his hand pressed against his new wound. As Darla came up, she jabbed the spear at Robert, missed, and got caught in the man's swing. He walloped her on the nose, and she fell over, landing on her back.

While Lawrence finished making his way up, Robert took off running. Grabbing his spear, Lawrence debated for a moment if he wanted to stab Darla, but he made his choice and moved on behind the house, following Robert. Darla shook her head, rolled over, and watched as the big man made his way into the darkness of the woods.

Floyd then came stumbling out, saw Martin hunched over, holding his injured arm, and then noticed Darla on her back. She saw Floyd and pointed in the direction of the woods. "They took the food," Darla said.

Floyd helped her up, debating on if it was worth heading into danger. He made his choice, taking off into the woods. "NO!" Darla cried to him, but Floyd kept on running.

As Robert entered the woods, he saw Lawrence, running as fast as he could—which wasn't all that quick. Robert waited, with a knife in one hand and a flashlight and pillowcase slung over his shoulder in the other. The big man finally got to him, out of breath. Robert had shoved the second flashlight into the front of his waistband. The handle popped over his shirt.

"Take it!" Robert demanded, and Lawrence snagged it and turned it on. As they began to run again, they heard footsteps tracking them. As Robert spun around, the flashlight cast a glow on Floyd. Lawrence aimed the spear at him.

"Give us some of the food back. We'll die if you don't!" Floyd begged.

"Fuck you," Robert said, turning around and taking off farther.

Lawrence heard Robert take off, leaving him to deal with Floyd alone.

"Wait for me," Lawrence said, but Robert was already gone.

Floyd stepped closer to Lawrence. He was holding his knife out with one hand, but his other hand was raised, palm facing the big man, signalling that he wanted this to be peaceful. "He only cares for himself, Lawrence, look."

Lawrence, sweaty and terrified, looked back and was unable to see Robert as he had already escaped into the darkness. "He's just going to leave you to die."

'Nah, he won't. We are just takin' off," Lawrence said.

"Let me pass, Lawrence; I need to get that food."

Lawrence, spear in one hand and flashlight in the other, kept it pointed at Floyd. He clearly wasn't sure what to do. Their plan wasn't going well, and Floyd, giving a ferocious glare at Lawrence, was shaking his head.

"Give me the flashlight, and I'll go after him. You head back to the house." But Lawrence shook his head no. There was a pause as both men looked at one another, then, Floyd cut around Lawrence, taking off after Robert.

"Hey!" Lawrence yelled and attempted to run after Floyd.

* * *

Martin gingerly lifted himself off the ground and headed back into the house, with Darla right behind him. "Get inside," he told her, and she did, then Martin attempted to casually close the door. Darla stopped him, sticking her hand in the way and pulling it back open.

Martin seemed surprised. "What are you doing?" he asked.

She looked at him with the same question. "What the hell are *you* doing?"

Martin reached for the door again with his right hand, grabbed hold, and attempted to push her out of the way to close it. "This needs to be shut," he said, with stress clear in his voice.

Darla interjected, keeping her feet planted on the ground. "Not without Floyd, Martin."

Martin shook his head, not believing her words. Darla could see what he was thinking just by his glare. Jolting into action, Martin held onto the door and tried again to push it shut, hoping to lock it tonight for good, but Darla blocked him again. He tried to shove her out of the way, even push her outside, but Darla did all she could to stop him and keep that door open.

"Stop! They'll be here soon, and they'll kill us!" he shouted in frustration.

"Not without Floyd!" Darla cried.

"But he's a dead man!" Martin shouted, and he continued to struggle.

* * *

Floyd followed the beam from the flashlight that Robert held. He was catching up to him. Floyd desperately wanted to yell at him to stop, but he was in a vulnerable position out in these woods armed with only a knife. His ego wasn't large enough to admit he could take those things out. He knew he couldn't, but he also knew that Robert or Lawrence couldn't either. But that didn't matter. Floyd had to grab the food because he knew the rations that were left just wouldn't be enough.

* * *

"Robert," a whispering voice said.

It stopped him in his tracks, and he looked to his left where the noise came from. Floyd heard Robert's name whispered too, yet he kept running towards him, seeing that he was now distracted. Robert slowly brought the light up the tree trunk next to him. Once it reached the top, Robert looked closer and saw a black box hoisted up top, barely hidden in the leaves.

Taking another step closer, he allowed himself to have a better look at the object, and then his name came from it again.

"Robert..."

Floyd tackled Robert face-first into the dirt, and the flashlight and knife flew from his hands. The bag of food landed to the right of them. Moving quickly, Floyd got himself up on top of Robert and punched the man in the back of his head. He gave three of his best blows to the back of the man's skull, as well as slamming his face into the cold dirt. Floyd's strength wasn't much, but he did what he could for the food. Getting himself off Robert, Floyd grabbed the pillowcase and began to run back. Robert was getting himself off the ground, and he started running after him.

"Stop him!" Robert called out, his voice echoing through the woods. Lawrence was coming up from behind, and he heard Robert's voice echoing over his heavy panting. As he did, he heard something cutting through the trees.

Taking a glance to his right, Lawrence saw Floyd high tailing it back to the house. "Fuck!" he cried. Then a horrid cry broke out from deep within the woods.

* * *

Martin had Darla by the hair, yanking her towards the floor with him, and she had her hands around his throat. With a great struggle, Darla was eventually able to get Martin onto his back, holding him there. With his foot, he tried to shove the door shut, knocking it with his toe. The door swung, but it wasn't strong enough to close it. Yet, it wouldn't take much more to finish the job.

Darla looked back, got off Martin, and reached for the handle, swinging it back open. As she did, Martin stood up behind her, wrapping his right arm around her neck, then he pulled her, dropping Darla on her back. He was still standing, pushing her down while reaching for the door.

It was a matter of quick thinking. Darla reached for his feet, pulled, and took Martin down, making him land on his stomach with his neck and head sticking out onto the porch. "FUCK!" he cried as his bodyweight fell on his injured and infected arm.

* * *

With Robert now surpassing Lawrence, Floyd was able to make his way out of the woods with the food. Floyd was now nearest to the house, coming around and heading to the front door, and Robert was next in line. The cries broke out again loud and clear through the night sky, and Robert saw the little girl storming towards him from the left. With his knife, he aimed it ready. The little girl let out a scream and jolted off her feet as she met him, taking him down on his back. Before he could react, she was on top of him, baring her teeth, thrashing and snapping those jaws of hers towards his face. Robert let out a scream. Floyd heard, turned back, and struggled to believe what he saw. As he stopped, he looked at them, then back at the house, then back toward Robert fighting for his life.

"Fuck," he said, hating the move he was about to make.

"Get off me, get off me!" Robert screamed, petrified. The creature didn't let up, though, still doing whatever it could to tear at his flesh. Robert saw the yellow eyes of death stare into his soul. This was it; this was his end. The next thing he knew, the pillowcase of food swung, hitting the girl in the side of her face, smacking her straight off Robert. Floyd then stepped over and stuck his knife in the nape of her neck.

The little girl let out a piercing cry into the night sky, almost as if she was calling for her mother's help. Floyd then kicked the little girl in the stomach for good measure as she thrashed around, struggling with the knife that protruded from her neck. He helped Robert up, almost regretfully, before taking the food and running back.

"Wait for me!" Lawrence cried out, but Floyd didn't hear him due to the events and his efforts at getting them back inside, but Robert did, and he turned around to see the big man still making a move for the house.

* * *

Martin pushed up from his stomach and struggled back into the house in front of the door, unable to get up from his knees. He then had Darla's arm around his neck, pulling him away. She was choking him out.

"We'll die," he struggled to say as Darla dropped to her back, holding him down. Then she saw his rotten arm, swaying as he tried to stop her from cutting off his breath, holding him from his objective.

As she was distracted, Martin elbowed her repeatedly, taking her breath away. He got up, grabbed the door with his right hand, and shoved it.

Floyd had just turned the corner, saw the door closing, and took two great leaps, reaching his left hand out and catching the sliver of space between the closing door and the frame. Floyd's knuckles crunched as he stopped the door, and he let out a scream.

Robert then drove his body towards the door, slamming the other side into Martin's face and knocking him on his back again. Robert came in stumbling, tripping over Martin and Darla and landing on the floor after colliding against the wall. Darla got up, saw Floyd still out on that porch, and slowly got up while holding his left hand tight. Crawling over, she grabbed him by his blazer collar and began to help him in. Floyd, with his feet, helped her by pushing himself in.

"Don't close it," Floyd said as he stumbled in. But Robert got up, pushed everyone aside, and shut the door. The lock slid sideways. As Robert took a breath, resting his head against the door, he saw what made his heart sink. The pillowcase of food, dropped by Floyd, lay outside on the porch. "No, no, no, no!" Robert yelled, slamming his hand against the window.

* * *

Lawrence headed back into the woods, the little girl running straight after him. He got back into the trees, moving as quickly as he could. There he saw the mother standing in front of him. Lawrence, unsure of what to do, held his spear out, sweating and shaking. "Come on, come on!" he roared with his last reserve of energy.

The little girl, the knife now out of her neck, came bolting for him. Her arms were out wide, and her razor-sharp fingernails were ready to slice and dice. She screamed as she went in for the kill. As she got close enough, Lawrence stuck the little girl in the shoulder and, with enough purchase, he lifted her and tossed her forcefully to the ground. He then turned around and made his way back toward the house again, praying the door was still open.

The mother came running; he could hear her approaching from behind. Lawrence, already too slow, stopped and spun around to jab the spear at his attacker. As he turned, he was greeted by a slash across his belly from her nails as she ran past him. Lawrence let out a cry, dropping to his knees from the breath-sucking pain. As he brought his eyes forward, the little girl ran past him, doing the same on the other side but running her fingers across his arms. The spear dropped beside him. With the slash across his arm, he was unable to pick up his weapon. Instead, Lawrence attempted to get up again and start running.

But the little girl was back, and she jumped on him from behind, latching her teeth onto his left side, tearing off his ear. Lawrence let out a scream as the girl jumped off him, swallowing what she'd removed. Lawrence dropped like the thud of a slain tree to the cold, hard dirt ground.

He trembled, doing what he could, still trying to crawl away. The little girl then slashed his back, and he let out another scream, feeling his flesh open up as blood gushed and ran down the sides of his body. His eyes caught gray, dead-like bare feet in front of him. As he brought his eyes toward the sky, Lawrence saw the mother in her bloody gown, staring at him with those piercing yellow eyes that would make anyone's blood run cold.

Flipping him onto his back, the mother got on her knees, holding his head between her legs. Lawrence tried to keep his eyes on her, grasping at his wound where his ear had been. "Please, God, please don't do this. Please don't do this. I'm so sorry for what I did. I'm so fuckin' sorr—"

The mother slashed Lawrence across the face. It felt like five box cutters had run across him at the same time with his left eye getting caught in the swipe. Lawrence tried to bring his head back up, but he only felt her cold, dead hands pressing him back down to the ground. She leaned in closer, staring into his eyes, and Lawrence could smell her stale, fetid breath. The little girl then got on top of Lawrence, tore open his gray sweater, and sank her jaws into his stomach. He tried to get away, but the mother held him down, smiling, and they stared at one another as the daughter tore into his guts.

33

Robert made his way back to the upper level to check the fridge. "That fat fuck put almost everything in that bag. Jesus Christ, we won't last a week." He then fell to his knees, unable to get a breath, in shock, trembling and sobbing.

Darla had her back against the left wall as did Floyd. Martin held his arm against his chest, with his bloody nose gushing from the impact of the door. Darla and Floyd could see the pillowcase of food laying on the porch right by the window. Darla began to cry with the frustration of seeing most of their food in that pillowcase outside. "We'll get it," Darla said, more to herself than anything, trying her best to stay optimistic.

"You fuck! You dropped the food!" Robert yelled from the kitchen to Floyd. But Floyd didn't respond. Getting up, Darla went right to the window, staring outside. She watched, waiting to see those things appear.

Floyd saw her. "What is it?" he asked, but she didn't respond.

Instead, Darla raised her fist and slammed it against the window. "Let us out! Let us out!" she begged, slamming it against the glass, again and again.

Floyd got up, approached her from behind, and grabbed a hold of her arm, bringing it to her side. "Please, stop," he said in her ear with a calming voice. Darla, crying, turned around and hugged him tightly.

"Jesus," Floyd said, losing his grip on her. She looked up and saw his eyes staring out the window. Turning around, Darla saw the horror that had caught his attention. Lawrence, still alive, stumbled to the ground near Jesse's body a few feet in front of the porch. Robert, who had begun pacing back and forth in the living room, caught sight too from the window. He pressed against the glass, watching from above as the women surrounded him.

He was alive but just barely so. Pushing himself onto his back, he revealed his facial wounds and his torn-up stomach, his intestines dangling beside him. The mother walked up to Lawrence, grabbed him by his head, and twisted his neck sideways. It was so fast, and the look of it was so painful, that they could almost hear his neck snap from inside. She then sunk her teeth into him, digging away.

"Oh no! Oh God, no!" Robert cried from upstairs. Darla turned away, unable to see anymore, but Floyd kept his eyes on the sight.

The little girl walked up to the porch, staring at Floyd from the other side of the window. Both were giving each other an expressionless glare. The little girl sniffed, looked down, saw the pillowcase, and got on top of it. Floyd walked up to the window and slammed his fist against the glass, trying to make as much noise as possible to distract her, but it was no use. "Don't do it," Floyd said underneath his breath. The little girl cut open the pillowcase, and dug in, savagely eating all the food that was left outside. Robert stepped in and saw this over Floyd's shoulder.

"No!" he shouted, pushing Floyd out of the way and slamming his palm against the window. Robert watched as the little girl ate their food while the mother feasted on the big man's corpse just a few feet away. He wanted to be sick.

Robert spun around with a violent glare at Floyd. When Floyd saw this, he took a step back, his hands up. Robert was shaking with rage. "You dropped the food out there. We'll starve because of you. We will starve!" Robert then made a move to attack, but Floyd swung a fist first, catching Robert on his left cheek. The hit wasn't much, but it was enough for Robert to lose his balance, misstep, and head down the stairs. Thankfully, for Floyd's sake, Robert knocked himself out as he collided against the wall, tumbling unconscious to the floor.

34

Martin was standing in the kitchen when Darla and Floyd confronted him. He was pouring himself a glass of water as Floyd grabbed him by the shoulder and spun him around. Martin, surprised by Floyd's aggressiveness, looked at him, nervous.

Floyd, with anger written all over his face, demanded an answer. "Was there a third envelope?" he asked. Martin shook his head.

"Use words," said Darla.

Martin stared at both of them. "Didn't you listen to me? I was only in my house last when the second envelope came. I don't know anything about a third."

"Are you lying to us?" Darla asked.

"Lying? About what?" Martin seemed confused.

"Do you have any idea why we're here? Now's the time for honesty," Floyd asked.

Martin shook his head. "No, I'm honest. I'm always honest."

"Did you kill Jesse?" Floyd asked.

"God, no, I couldn't do that to someone."

"If you're lying, we will find out," Floyd said.

Darla and Floyd looked at one another, then stepped away from Martin. His injured arm was behind his back, and Darla noticed this, and both noticed his missing tooth. Floyd walked over to the refrigerator and opened the doors, taking a gander at what was left. Darla saw Martin was trying to hide his arm, but she remembered what it looked like when they were fighting. As she was about to ask Martin to see it, Floyd spoke up. "We've got some pork left, a little bit of lettuce, and one slice of bread. Two more days' worth—if we ration small."

Darla had her eyes on Martin as she backtracked towards the fridge to have a look, but Martin took off past them, saying, "Goodnight," and heading all the way to Room 7. The door was heard swinging shut—then silence. Floyd and Darla looked at one another. Floyd was confused at Martin's behaviour.

"What was that?" he asked.

Darla leaned over to look down the hallway, saw that no one was there, then kept to a whisper. "His arm. I saw it when we had our little wrestling match, it's—"

"Wrestling match?" Floyd was confused.

"He tried to shut the door while you guys were out there. I stopped it—with force. When I had him on the ground, I saw his arm. It's infected. Badly."

"We should have a look," Floyd said.

'We will. He can't try and hide it from us for long."

Darla then noticed Floyd's hand. "Jesus, look at that."

He snapped it away. "It's fine."

35

Floyd walked to the middle section, holding a glass of water. Down below was Robert, still out cold, with the top half of his body lying on the floor and his waist and legs resting on the stairs. Floyd, resting his glass of water on the floor, took the stairs softly, quietly making his way around Robert to not wake him. Once in the basement, Floyd got down on one knee, looking closer at the unconscious son of a bitch. Floyd took a breath, reached his hands over, and gently, he pinched Robert's nose with his good hand and covered his mouth with his busted one.

Robert's breathing stopped its regular pattern, and his body struggled for air. Floyd held Robert's fingers and mouth tight. The unconscious man began to shake gently. His eyes were half opening, then closing, and his face was no longer red but pale—and on the eve of becoming blue. Floyd's hands began to shake, guilt eating at him. He wanted to kill Robert for many reasons, but food, to him, was the main purpose. If there was anyone Floyd felt didn't deserve to eat, it was Robert.

Robert's feet began to thrash as his boots began to dance on the steps. The breathing, the choking noises, all of it, felt like a stick, jabbing into Floyd's neck. He tried to hold on, but the longer he did, the louder everything seemed to get.

He let go, standing up. As he did, it felt like everything had gone silent. Had he done it?

Stepping over, his heart beating quickly, he was unsure. Taking a closer look, he saw Robert's chest suddenly rise, then deflate. Floyd paced around, shaking off what he had just attempted. Then, leaving Robert where he lay, Floyd went back up the stairs and grabbed his water, shaking as he drank.

36

In the middle of the night, in Room 7, Martin curled up in bed, his stomach aching with a pain he'd never felt before. It was as if he'd swallowed needles, and they were now swimming around, jabbing all his insides. Then, Martin felt the urge to throw up again, and he stumbled out of his room. He went back to that horrid toilet and projectile vomited into the bowl, with backwash and spray getting on him and everything nearby. More built up in his stomach, soon heading up, then out of his mouth. After it happened a second time, he dropped to his back and lay on the cold floor for a moment. An intense need for food then followed.

Martin knew he shouldn't eat right now— especially their food—but he felt he had no other choice. Opening the bathroom door slowly, he peeked his head out, saw that it was clear, and headed to the kitchen. Once he was there, he, very slowly and with caution wanting to make as little sound as he could, opened the fridge doors. There, he took the last slice of bread and shoved it in his mouth. His eyes shut with just the sheer pleasure of eating. Swallowing it, he felt how slow it was going down. He then walked over to the jug of water and unscrewed the lid. Lifting it, Martin began to chug the water down.

When he was done, he placed the jug on the counter, only then realizing that he may have drunk way too much, which wouldn't seem fair. But it was too late. His stomach felt somewhat settled. Bringing his infected arm up, he took a look and saw how much worse it was getting. He knew he could be changing into one of them—maybe their bites were poisonous—but he preferred to remain in denial. Maybe it was only a terrible infection that he hoped would soon be checked by a doctor. Martin, wanting a better look, turned himself around so he wouldn't have his back to the kitchen light any longer.

With his eyes still on his wound, he turned. As he did, a knife drove into his stomach, taking his breath away. His focus went from the wound on his arm that he held to a hand holding a knife that was now in him. Martin dropped his infected arm, and it swung like a stick on a rope. He was face to face with Robert. The man had blood dripping down from a cut from his forehead, trickling down to his scruffy beard. Robert had a look that was driven by anger.

"Stealing food, are we?" Robert said, and he grabbed Martin's neck with his left hand, pulled the knife out of his stomach with his right, and struck Martin in the stomach again. Robert pulled Martin closer, breathing into his ear. "Taker's justice," he whispered, then stabbed Martin for a third time.

Grasping onto Robert's beard, Martin held it tight, resting his chin on Robert's left shoulder. Choking noises came from him as Robert held the blade in his guts, twisting and turning it, hearing the blood drip from Martin's stomach to the kitchen floor.

Martin's last thought was about how Robert had a knife. He thought he had left it outside. Strange, he knew, but as his mind puzzled, Robert stuck him again in the stomach, pushed him back, took the blade out, and stuck Martin in the neck to finish him off. Once he pulled the knife out for the final time, Martin's knees buckled, yet he still held onto Robert's beard. As he fell, his hand let go, and then he finally dropped lifeless to the floor.

Robert, took in a slow, meditative breath as he stood above Martin, calming his heart rate. Seeing the body lying on his side, Robert stepped out of the way of the kitchen light so that he could take a better look at Martin. Robert, for the first time, saw the infected arm, then caught notice of the blood. It wasn't red, it was black, and it was pooling out towards his feet as he hunched over close to the body. Robert took a step back, examining the corpse. He'd seen nothing like it before.

37

Morning came, and Darla and Floyd were lying in Room 5. Floyd was awake—he had been most of the night. He was staring at his now-busted fingers. The light from outside washed over them from the small bedroom window, and Floyd couldn't help but keep staring, spinning his hand around, fascinated by the injury and how it made his hand look.

"Floyd," a voice said.

Beyond his feet at the base of the bed, Floyd saw the living room of his old cottage. There, his mother sat, young and healthy. She was staring at him, smiling, and so he smiled back.

"Hey, Mom, you look so happy."

His mother chuckled. "I am, sweetheart."

She had a newspaper in one hand and a coffee in the other. Placing the paper on the table, she leaned back and held onto her coffee with both hands. "Been having a rough week?" she asked with concern, frowning, almost pouting.

Floyd chuckled and shook his head. "You have no idea. We don't know what to do."

"Well, what have I always told you?"

Floyd shrugged.

"If something isn't going well, and it doesn't seem to be getting any better, then just quit and say good riddance," his mother said, then took a sip of her coffee.

"Can you open the door for us, Mom?"

His mother shook her head. "After what you did, no way."

Darla woke up in a sweat, snapping Floyd out of his hallucination. He was concerned, seeing what Darla seemed to be going through. He rested his hand on her back. Her breathing was savage as she stared towards the wall. "Calm down; it's okay," he said, trying to ease her, but Darla just kept breathing heavy and muttering the same words. Her eyes went misty, tears trickled down her face, and her right hand rested on her stomach, rubbing in circles.

Floyd leaned in. "Darla?"

But her attention never went to him. "How could I forget, how could I? What the hell is wrong with me? It's not possible. I have no signs, how could it be possible?" she said out loud, yet not to Floyd but herself.

"Hey, Darla, forget about what? What's not possible?"

Darla didn't respond to him again and continued talking to herself. "How could I? They made this happen,

Darla. They made you forget. This place, they made you forget. You have to leave. You have to leave." More tears came down. This time Darla lost it, sobbing into her palms as she covered her face.

"Jesus, Darla, what is it? Please talk to me," Floyd begged her.

Darla took a breath, a break between her cries. "We have to leave tonight, we, we, we, c-can't wait here any longer," she said, and then she went back to crying.

Floyd nodded. "Okay, okay, we will. Please, how can I help you? Tell me what to do right now."

Darla shook her head, her voice breaking through her cries. "It's not possible. How could I forget?"

Floyd's heart raced. "Darla, forget what? Please talk to—"

"I'm pregnant!"

38

Floyd was speechless. His mind was too broken to come up with the right words. Darla went back to sobbing, doing what she could to catch her breath.

"H-how?" Floyd said.

She stopped and turned to him, frowning. "What?" she asked.

Floyd took a deep breath. "How do you, how do you forget something like that?"

But after he asked the question, Darla continued crying, unable to answer. The guilt overwhelmed her. Floyd slipped off the bed, then went around to the door, trembling. Darla looked up at him. "Don't leave. Please," she begged. Floyd stopped moving, his hand on the doorknob.

He turned to her. "I-I need a glass of water." Floyd opened the door and stepped out, shutting it behind himself.

Standing in the hallway, Floyd shivered. Opening his blazer, he stuck his hand in, pulled out his broken glasses, and placed them back on his face. He could sort of see through the left lens that had a deep crack down the centre. He had his hand against the wall, trying to hold himself up. His knees felt weak from the lack of food and drink, shaking as they took on the weight of the situation. Moving out of the hallway, Floyd kept his hand on the wall as he dragged his feet to the end. There he saw Robert, sitting, twirling a knife that seemed to be covered in some kind of black tar.

Their eyes met, and Robert smiled at Floyd.

"Good morning," Robert said kindly, and he gave Floyd a wave.

Floyd's right eye caught sight of the body in the kitchen straight after, and he found himself speechless once again, seeing the mess on the floor and Martin, lifeless, splayed out on his side. Robert stood, the knife still gripped tightly in his hand as he stared at Floyd. "He was stealing food. So, I did what was right."

"My God, Robert," Floyd said.

"Something was wrong with him too. Those demons gave him a disease. His blood is thicker than normal and blacker than the night sky."

Floyd took a few steps back, and Robert tilted his head, looking at him. "What's wrong there, Floyd? You scared? I'm not going to hurt you. We're in this together." Floyd shook while he stood still, watching Robert. He could see in his eyes and smile that the man just wasn't right. His voice had a creeping insanity underneath its tone. A mind now cracked.

Robert took a step forward, twirling his knife, the tip of the blade cutting into the end of his right index finger. Floyd noticed as a small amount of blood began to drip while Robert didn't even bat an eye at what he was doing to himself. He just kept that smile. "If we want to survive this then we all have to play fair. We're their dolls in this house. You'd agree?" Robert asked.

Floyd, for the sake of it, nodded in agreement.

Robert shrugged his shoulders in delight. "Great. Now, go ahead and get what you need."

39

Robert killed Martin," Floyd said in a whisper. Darla's stomach turned in knots upon hearing the news. She sat up in bed, her face tense, eyes darting at Floyd. "I don't care how we get out of here. If we have to go to the shore and eat god damn seagulls, I'll do it."

Floyd was leaning against the wall, arms crossed, thinking of their next move. "Robert is starting to lose it, he's saying weird shit." Floyd told her.

Darla glared at him, confused. "Like what?"

Floyd moved to the bed and took a seat. "He was off, the way he was speaking to me, said we're dolls in a dollhouse. He had his knife digging into his finger, seemed to not even notice."

Darla didn't say anything for a moment, her face blank, only giving subtle nods, and then she looked at Floyd and said, "He didn'—"

"Like he felt nothing," Floyd said, beginning to giggle from the insanity of it all. Darla didn't.

There was a pause, and then Darla rested her hand on Floyd's arm. Looking at him, with sorrow in her eyes, she said, "We have to kill him. He's a danger and always has been."

Floyd agreed, yet he only nodded. Darla stood up, hands resting on her belly. "My thoughts are that whatever they used to get us here is the reason why I forgot about the baby."

"Still, who put us here?" Floyd asked.

"Who the hell knows?"

"A little while ago, you said you thought this could be supernatural since we were thinking about Martin and the seven deadly sins. I hate to say it, but maybe it's true. This may be some kind of purgatory for us. It's none of my business, but, Darla, have you done anything wrong—in the major sense. A serious crime?"

Darla turned to him, shaking her head, feeling a little disrespected by his question. "How could you ask me that. No, of course not!" she snapped.

"I'm sorry. It's just those things out there are something I'd felt like I've seen before. Somehow. Maybe in some old painting or religious book. They just, feel so familiar the longer I'm here. Maybe it's their presence that I've felt before. Can't put a finger on it."

"I agree," Darla said.

"You do?"

"Yeah, I feel something about them. You're not crazy. The more the days go by, the more I feel like some part of this seems 'familiar', and I can't explain to myself why."

She paused.

"Did we get another envelope?"

Floyd shook his head. "No, I didn't see one—unless Robert snagged it."

Darla nodded. "I'm going to see my children again, Floyd, and I'm going to see the one that's inside me too one day. Nothing is going to stop me."

ACT III

40

In the kitchen, Darla arrived and saw Martin's body for the first time—they had lost track of time, sitting in the bedroom. It was a bloody mess, and it lay there as stiff as bark as Darla walked up to examine it. Her heart sank at the sight of him, and she went to the table and breathed deeply. Floyd had taken the food that remained out of the fridge and placed it on the table, sliding some over for Darla. Pork, lettuce…and that was it. Sitting together on the opposite end of the refrigerator, Darla and Floyd ate in silence. As Darla ate her pork, finishing it quickly, she glanced at Martin again, his stiff corpse lying still, and she felt nothing but sorrow for him.

"2026 has been a rough year hasn't it," Floyd said with a chuckle as he ate.

Darla stopped, then turned to Floyd with a frown. Swallowing her food, Darla paused and stared at Floyd. He turned and looked at her, tilting his head in confusion and stopped his chewing. Darla leaned in, keeping that glare of confusion.

"It's 2029."

"Don't kid with me right now," Floyd said, giving Darla a blank stare.

"It's not 2026, I can assure you. For a fact."

Floyd shook his head. "Before I woke up here, Darla, it was 2026. *I know* that for a fact."

There was a moment of pause.

"Well shit… I-I can't explain that," Darla said, turning away from him, trying to think.

"This is hell," Floyd said with shock in his eyes.

A soft noise arose, and their attention was caught. Martin's body began to breathe.

41

As his stomach rose and deflated, Darla glared at the body with her eyes wide. Floyd kept eating, unaware of the situation until Darla knocked him on the shoulder. "Floyd, I thought he was dead."

He frowned, mouth full of food, and turned to her. When he did, Floyd saw Martin breathing in and out. Some chewed-up pork fell from his mouth as his jaw dropped. "Christ almighty!"

Darla rose from her seat, her nerves jangling. Floyd stepped away and came around the opposite side of the kitchen counter.

Darla came close to the body, stepping around black, tar-like blood that drained to the floor. His breathing intensified. It was as if, at first, Martin had received some kick-start boost, then his breathing got back into a natural rhythm.

"Martin? Martin?" Darla said, but no response came. The body lay there, eyes shut, the only difference its breathing.

"He's alive?" Floyd muttered, and Darla turned to him, swallowing some of those jangled nerves.

"I don't think he really is," she said.

Floyd took a step around, leaning over the corpse and staring. "You don't think he is? The guy is fucking breathing." Floyd then bent down to help Martin, the shock still there.

Darla reached out, grabbed his arm, and tugged Floyd towards her. "Don't touch him. He's infected."

"He's breathing, Darla; this may be our—"

"Don't be a fucking idiot. The guy isn't the same now as he was. Hell, the fucker wasn't healthy when we let him in here. Don't touch him. I don't want to lose you, too."

"So, what? We just leave him?"

"No." Darla turned to the clock and then back towards Floyd. "We leave him here. Take off when the time comes. All the more reason to leave."

Floyd took another glance, seeing that Darla was most likely right. Floyd bent over and had a closer look. "Floyd, don't."

As Darla reached over to stop him, Floyd swatted her hand away. Taking a step back, she couldn't bear the suspense as he leaned in close, reaching his hand out towards

254

Martin's face. Lifting his upper lip, Floyd saw that Martin now had razor-sharp teeth. Then, lifting Martin's eyelid, saw that his eyes were dark yellow. As Floyd stood, he stepped away, turning to Darla and saying, "We're going to have a big problem very soon."

42

Darla had Martin by the ankles, and Floyd had his wrists. Walking down the hallway, they brought him to Room 7. Laying Martin on the floor, Darla took the bedsheets and tore strips with her knife, using them to tie Martin's hands together around the bed post. Not a fuss came from him as she did so, and once finished, Darla, with Floyd, left the bedroom, shutting the door behind them.

43

Darla and Floyd held each other tight, sitting in the living room, both with a knife in hand. The ticking of the clock felt like a stick jabbing in their eardrums. The stench from the bathroom no longer stayed put, and it drifted its way to the living room.

Martin was in Room 7 with the door shut. The plan was to leave the house, with Martin still inside. Darla leaned over and saw that they had seven minutes 'til the lock opened. Floyd stood as Darla did; both were fed—at least, as close to that as possible—and ready to leave with the remaining water.

Floyd took a stride forward, but Darla caught him. They met each other's eyes. Darla smiled, pulled him close, and slowly, she kissed him. She held the kiss until the door opened. They turned towards the noise, and both saw Robert walking out of the hallway, no shirt and no shoes, standing barefoot and confused.

"What the fuck are you two doing?" he asked.

Floyd aimed his knife at Robert, who had no weapon, it seemed, on him. "We're leaving, Robert."

Robert shook his head. "No, no, you can't leave. You open that door, death comes. You're both just going to leave and die." Robert spoke in an almost childish tone.

Floyd and Darla both moved closer to Robert, keeping their blades aimed high. Walking past him while facing the son of a bitch, they didn't want to lose sight of him. They backtracked towards the door, but Robert followed them, shaking his head, becoming more outraged by the second. He then began thrashing his arms, furious, unable to contain his anger.

"You would just leave me. You fucks! You'd just leave me here. You'll die out there. It's not safe. Fucking fools."

"Robert, please," Darla said, her weaponless hand raised to ease him. "Once this door opens, we'll be gone. You will never have to deal with us again."

"No, you can't leave. You can't fucking leave!

"BANG!"

The noise resonated from down the hallway. Martin, the infected soul, began banging his clenched hands against the inside of the door. His breathing suddenly stopped, and he let out a cry.

Robert turned away from the noise and back toward Darla and Floyd. "What the fuck was that?"

"How much goddamn time left, Floyd?" Darla asked.

"I don't know."

"What the fuck was that noise?" Robert barked.

Darla and Floyd, knives still aimed toward Robert, pressed themselves against the door. Darla, with her free hand, twisted the lock, hoping to God that it opened soon. "Come on, come on, come on."

Martin's fists violently flailed against the bedroom door.

Robert's head spun back and forth. "What the fuck is that?" Leaving them for a moment, Robert ran to the hallway. He looked on as Room 7's door shook as whatever was inside desperately tried to break out. Stepping over to the railing, Robert stood watching Darla twist the door's lock, begging to be free. Floyd kept his blade pointing at Robert.

"He's turned and you're leaving me with that thing!" Robert cried.

Martin's violent rampage continued echoing down the hallway as his fists slammed against the wooden door.

BANG!

BANG!

BANG!

BANG!

BANG!

BANG!

BANG!

BANG!

The noise was unbearable. Robert stepped closer. "You fucks. You fucks!"

"Stay back!" Floyd demanded.

Martin, thrashing and slamming his fists, began throwing his body against the door. His face was pressed up against the cold wood, his razor-sharp teeth were out, ready to tear, and he whipped his head back and forth. Martin smashed his head into the door. Again, and again and again. The creature heard their voices and wanted nothing more than to feast on them.

It was coming for them and would escape soon. As Floyd brought his gaze back to Robert, it met the man's fist, and the power of the blow knocked Floyd up against the window. While dazed, Darla took a jab at Robert, stabbing him in the arm. Though it was deep, Robert didn't seem to notice. Grabbing her hair, Robert made sure every root felt his strength. The blade slipped out of Robert's flesh and dropped to the floor in a bloody mess.

The door of Room 7 began to break apart. The destruction echoed down the hallway.

He tossed Darla across to the other wall, and she slid and hit her head. Stepping closer, Robert looked down at

Darla as she glared back at him, raising her hands in defence. "Fucking cunt!" he screamed.

The knife sunk into Robert's side, and he saw Floyd with his bruised, blood-drenched face, holding a knife. Latching onto Floyd's wrist, Robert twisted it counterclockwise, and Floyd's face shook in pain as he tried not to scream. But when his arm went too far, he howled. Floyd, trapped, now only with his busted left hand free, did all he could by flailing his broken hand against Robert's shoulder. Darla, reaching for her knife by Robert's feet, caught hold of the handle and stuck the blade into his left calf, retracting the blade, then sticking him in the upper left thigh in one swift movement.

"Fuck!" Robert cried, and he tossed Floyd down the stairs towards the bottom level, and with a knee-jerk reaction, he swung his opposite foot and kicked Darla in the face. Floyd flew down the steps, landing in a daze, and Darla, her back against the wall and still lying on the floor, watched as Robert held onto his new wound, even starting to sob from the pain.

The lock slid up, and Darla was the first to see it. She crawled towards the door, getting up to her knees and latching onto the handle. Robert swung his head around, and in great panic, he cried out, "Don't fucking leave me!"

Darla swung the door open, knife still in her hand, and Robert limped after her, checking her to the porch. As

Robert landed on her, the sound of sunken flesh rang out as her blade entered into him. Darla opened her eyes to meet Robert's who'd gone wide. She felt blood trickle down her neck, but it wasn't hers. Robert, pushing himself off her, trembled as he stood with Darla's knife stuck in his chest. His hands clasped the blade, but he had no strength to remove it.

Backtracking towards the house, Robert fell to one knee in the middle of the doorway. Standing tall, she looked down on Robert with her battered face, smiled, then walked over and pulled the blade out slowly, making sure he felt every inch escape. The man couldn't speak, and he only gurgled blood as she pulled the knife out. Their eyes met, then she drove the blade into his throat.

An ear-drum-bursting cry broke out.

Darla's eyes shot up and saw Martin, now free, a few steps away inside. Closing in on Darla's final moment of vengeance. The creature, arms full and jaws ready, ran and took out Robert as he still was on one knee with the knife still in his throat. Darla jumped out of the way. The demon drove itself into Robert, tackling him off the porch and out onto the dirt and grass. Darla ran inside and slammed the door shut.

44

She dragged Floyd from the bottom of the steps and into the basement. Darla, exhausted and beaten, then took a seat, holding Floyd in her lap, his back against her stomach. He was in a daze, murmuring words Darla was unable to make out. Holding him tightly, she kissed his cheek. "Tomorrow, we leave," she said, letting the tears flow.

Floyd held onto her arm, murmuring again. Darla leaned in, whispering, "He's gone. Robert is gone now. He won't hurt us or stop us any longer. It's over. Just the two of us now, Floyd."

Floyd, in a daze, looked up at Darla. Blood trickled down his forehead, and his eyes were squinting, trying to get the best look at her. "You… y-you saved me."

Darla smiled, holding him tight. "And you saved me." Wiping the blood from his head, Darla leaned down and kissed Floyd, then pulled back and shut her eyes to rest.

45

Floyd was the first to wake. Getting up, he felt Darla's arms around him. Gently raising them and making his way out of her warm grasp, Floyd stood up, quietly not wanting to disturb her as she slept soundly on the floor. As he arrived upstairs, Floyd went to the kitchen and saw the jug of water on the counter that he had forgotten to take from Robert. Unscrewing the cap, he lifted the jug of water up and drank as much as he could, leaving the rest for Darla. Tonight had to be the night, as, after today, both would be out of water for good.

Checking the counter, another envelope rested in its usual place. Floyd didn't skip a beat, rushing over, slicing the top, and pulling the letter out, desperately wanting to read the message. Tossing the yellow envelope to the floor with a sad face on the top, Floyd unfolded the letter, reading what it said. It read:

9pm, watch that clock.

Flipping the letter over, Floyd was hoping for more words on the paper. But that was it—that simple, disappointing message. *Then what?* he thought. But Floyd, like with everything these past days, had no real answers. A wave of anger and frustration flooded over him. His fuse was short. His hand crumpled the paper, and he began to laugh hysterically with rage hidden underneath. He continued to laugh, tossing the paper across the living room towards the clock. Floyd went silent as the crumpled yellow ball bounced off the clock, landing on the sofa.

Walking over to it, Floyd took notice of the ticking. Each tick, making him twitch as he came closer. "Tick-tick-tick-tick-tick, that's all you do, huh? Just *tick* all goddamn day. Don't you get sick of it?"

Floyd stopped and stood in front of the clock, watching the second-hand beat. Floyd was rocking back and forth to the tick with no realization that he was.

TICK. TICK. TICK. TICK.

"Shut up," Floyd said softly to the clock.

TICK. TICK. TICK. TICK. TICK. TICK. TICK. TICK. TICK.

"I said, shut up."

TICK. TICK. TICK. TICK. TICK.

"Shut up, shut up," Floyd said, now tugging on his hair.

TICK. TICK.

"I said shut up. I. Said. Shut. Up."

TICK.

"Please, just stop. Just…just…just stop, okay? Please?" Floyd put his hands together as if he were praying. Tears were now trickling down his cheeks.

TICK. TICK.

"I was rude… I was… I'm just asking you to politely to stop making noise. Please."

TICK. TICK.

His hands were now shaking, clasping onto his hair with his right hand as he paced around the living room.

TICK. TICK. TICK. TICK.

"Fuck you!"

Floyd then ran and began smashing both his busted and healthy hand against the glass of the clock. Tears were now streaming as he desperately pleaded, "Please, God, please, I'm sorry. I'm sorry, for what I did. I'm so sorry!"

Floyd then dropped to his knees, still hearing the ticking from above. Floyd curled up into a ball, rocking back and forth. "Stop!" he yelled into his lap.

A hand rested on his shoulder, and Floyd spun around. There, Darla stood, looking down at him. Though she'd had bruises all over her body from the hell she'd gone through, and even though his sight was a bit of a blur when her caring smile shined down on him, Floyd thought she was the most beautiful woman he'd ever seen. The ticking from the clock seemed to go away as soon as he lost focus on it as he stared into her eyes. He got up, and they wrapped each other's arms around one another.

* * *

Floyd and Darla, both in bed together, held each other tight. Lying down comfortably, Floyd faced the door. He wasn't sure what number bedroom they were in anymore; his sight couldn't quite make out the number. They were both exhausted, falling asleep off and on, and then they usually woke each other up with stomach growls or sudden twitches.

"We, w-we should make weapons," Darla said, still lying down with her eyes shut. Floyd smacked his lips, feeling how dry they were, amazed at how dehydrated he was even after drinking recently.

"We have a knife still," Floyd said.

"One knife? Or more?"

"J-just one. I counted."

"Where is it?" Darla asked.

"You had it last," Floyd said.

It was true. She remembered she left it on the top step of the stairs leading to the basement. While letting out a breath, Darla's anxiety spiked when Floyd said she was the last to have it—she didn't want that responsibility. She smiled, even laughing at the relief. The fog in both of their minds was thick. Darla could feel her sanity slipping by the hour, and Floyd could feel it as well. But neither wanted to mention it.

"Why bother now?" Darla mumbled.

"What?" Floyd asked, but Darla didn't respond.

"You thinking of the clock?" Darla asked Floyd, resting her hand on his left cheek.

"I hate that clock."

"What do you think the message meant, Floyd?"

"I-I don't know."

"Think it's dangerous?"

Floyd's eyes opened, and he sat up in the bed; his heart began to pound in his chest. He could hear it. Clasping onto his shirt, Floyd began to panic as his breathing started to rev up. "You think so?" he asked, and Darla sat up.

"I don't know."

Floyd shot a look away. Only then did he see he had a tear in his blazer. "Damn it," he said.

Darla rested her arm on his shoulder. "What is it?"

"I've got a rip on my sleeve."

"It doesn't matter. I-it doesn't matter, Floyd."

"But it does."

"Why?"

"'Cause, it does."

Floyd then turned to Darla and smiled. "I was thinking, you know, this whole place. It's not much d-different than home. You know?"

"What? It's nothing…like it, Floyd."

He shook his head from side to side. "Think about it. Humans are placed on Earth, with no real understanding of how we got here. The planet has dangers all around—things we still can't explain. There are creatures that want to kill us, limited food and water, and power struggles between us—stupid, hairless apes, that's what we are. What the hell is the difference?"

Darla saw his point, yet she had too much fog in her brain to engage in his comments. "Yeah, maybe, but what I don't have here, Floyd, are my children. That is what I'm missing."

Floyd reached over and kissed Darla, slowly and softly, but then he snapped himself back. He was shaking his head.

Darla saw he was hesitant. "What's wrong? she asked.

Floyd smiled, placing his right hand on his head. "I'm sorry," he said.

Darla leaned over, clasped onto his blazer, and gently pulled him closer. Both looked at one another, and then they kissed again.

46

It was 8:58 pm when Darla and Floyd walked into the living room. Both sat on the sofa across from the clock. As they sat down, Floyd, with his working hand, held onto Darla's. They smiled at one another, then sat in silence, watching the second-hand tick its final two minutes away. When the time was nearly up, they gripped each other a little tighter, and then the second hand reached twelve. The lock downstairs slid north as it always did, and Darla and Floyd heard the noise, turning their heads towards it. Floyd wanted to stand, but Darla squeezed his hand a little tighter. As he looked at her, she shook her head. "Wait for a—"

A cracking noise came from the clock, and both Darla and Floyd turned towards the sound. The second hand had stopped moving when the cracking began. It was faint, but the sounds grew.

Shoooook, shoook, shoooook, shoook, shook, shook, shook, shook, shook, shook.

Chug!

The clock then extended out of the wall. Darla and Floyd saw this and pressed themselves against the back of the couch, eyes glued to what was happening. The clock then dropped down, still attached to the bottom, and lay flat, straight outwards like a murphy bed. There was a hole and darkness beyond. Darla had the knife with her, and she was gripping it tightly, ready for anything. A strange noise grew from the darkness, and out extended a small television attached to a mechanical arm.

'What?" Darla said.

The television stopped, and a blank screen stared at the two of them across on the couch. Seconds passed and nothing. Holding each other's hands even tighter, Darla and Floyd stayed where they were, hearts beating, eyes staring. But only silence followed. Floyd nudged her on the shoulder. "You thi—"

The television turned on, showing only static. This lasted for a few more seconds before a black and white image appeared—a backdrop of one that resembled a stage. Floyd couldn't see it. "Wha—"

"Shhhhhhh," Darla said.

A man walked on camera, no music, only footsteps. He could be seen head to toe. Black jacket, pants, shoes, and a tie with a white shirt. With slicked back hair and a cigarette in his hand, he smiled at the two of them and walked closer to the camera, the frame cutting off his waist and legs once he did so.

He took a puff of his cigarette and then smiled. "Darla and Floyd, congratulations." He paused. "You two have been through quite the journey these past few days, haven't you? By God, I'm sure you're now at your wit's end. This has been some of the best entertainment we've had on this show since its birth. On behalf of myself and the crew of this show, and for the viewers at home, we want to thank you for such wonderful entertainment." The man smiled and put his cigarette back in his mouth, giving the two of them applause. He was followed by what sounded like an applause track behind him.

"What the hell is this shit?" Floyd muttered.

The man stopped clapping as did the track. Taking his cigarette out of his mouth, he smiled, gave a wink, then with the fingers that held his smoke, he pointed towards the camera. "You two are begging for some answers, I'm sure, which, you'll be getting very shortly. It's been fun for us, Darla and Floyd, to watch you both make it so far. The bond you've created. The triumphs you've made. This whole experience has been so satisfying. Watching Phillip get what he deserved. Watching, you, Floyd, sneak off and kill Ken while he slept, then turning the tables on Robert. Oh, and Robert, what a son of a gun."

Darla turned to Floyd, letting go of his hand, and stared at him as his face tensed as he kept his eyes on the TV.

"Then, another contestant, Martin, survived his escape, only to land at your house. My God, the drama! The viewers loved it. I know I did. Things only got juicier from there. Paranoia grew, and Robert's mind started to crack. Did you see how he manipulated Jesse and Lawrence? The most gruesome bit was how Robert blinded Jesse and cut his throat, only to blame the murder on the new guy. Then there was when Lawrence was left for dead by you, and then Robert was eaten alive by the infected." The presenter took another puff. "Oh, and then, of course, Robert getting a knife in the neck by you, Darla—that was great TV. Crazy times."

Darla felt sick as she sat up from the couch, nauseous from what she was hearing.

"Now, of course, this season viewers wanted to try something new—a competition to see what the differences would be if, with one house we had six females and one male, and yours, of course, with six males and one female. It was fascinating to see the differences in the dynamics. This season's theme was brought to us after many votes—and it was the 7 deadly sins.

All of you were chosen due to the crimes you committed that related to each sin. Phillip was Pride—killing a child while looking in the mirror while driving, then speeding off.

Ken—Wrath—beating a child after losing his temper. Then there was Jesse, accidentally killing his daughter by ever slowly poisoning her for donation money from those who felt sorrow for her—just so he wouldn't have to work. Lawrence, Gluttony, whose overindulgence in alcohol caused him to crack a young student's skull open during an altercation. Oh, and that monster Robert, what he tried to do to those poor young girls. Hell, even his wife took a shot at him. Didn't kill him though, just a graze. I'm sure he wished he went that way instead. Deserved it, everything he got. Now, I must ask, have you two spoken to each other about your crimes? I'm going to assume it's a no."

Darla turned to Floyd with sadness overwhelming her. "What did you do, Floyd?"

"I should ask you the same," he said, not letting his eyes leave the screen.

The presenter smiled. "It's been a great game to watch you all play. But it's not over yet. Dollhouse requires there to be only one winner left alive. No, ifs, ands, or buts. One winner. Let the best player win. Cheers, you two, and best of luck." The television then shut off and backtracked into the wall. The two sat and watched as it sunk back into the darkness. After it was gone, they sat in silence, doing what they could to process the situation.

"I hope you were all entertained!" Floyd screamed.

Darla began to sob. Taking in a breath, Floyd looked at Darla, staring as she cried. Resting his hand on her back, she pulled herself away. Bringing her now wet eyes to him. "Is it true, did you kill Ken?" Floyd sighed, then looked away from her, unable to allow Darla to see the shame of it all. "We do what we have to do to survive."

Darla brought her teary eyes away from Floyd, taking in another breath. "I'm just so sick of it all, Floyd, I still don't understand anything that's going on. I don't—"

Taking the knife from her loose grip, without a second's pause, he sunk the blade into Darla's stomach. The breath from her body escaped her. Turning back and looking at Floyd. He sat, shame in his wet eyes, shaking his head at her as he held the blade into her now bloody guts.

"I'm so sorry, Darla dear. I'm so, so sorry."

DARLA

Darla came into the room dressed in an orange jumper, her hands cuffed in front of her with her ankles chained as well. In the room was a woman—tall, slim, and dressed in business attire with a face that had a strong, beautiful intense structure and bright red hair. She sat confidently yet innocently. She had a look that showed compassion and empathy, yet you knew she could tear your head off corporately. The woman had a clipboard and a pen in front of her, and she followed Darla as she took a seat on the metal chair.

The woman took her eyes off Darla for a moment, smiling, to address the guard that brought her in the room. "You can step out. I've got it from here."

Turning to Darla, she smiled, though it never reached her eyes. "You're not going to cause any trouble, are you, Darla?"

Keeping her eyes on the woman, Darla didn't speak, she only shook her head.

"Great," the woman said with glee. The guard stepped out of the room, yet he stayed near the door.

'What's this about?" Darla asked, resting her cuffed hands on the table.

The woman didn't respond at first, only bringing the clipboard with papers closer to her eyes. On the corner was a picture of Darla's mug shot, and then all her information was underneath. She watched as the woman's eyes scanned the paper, slowly going down, reading the information over again for a quick refresher.

"Hello, Darla, my name is Lacy Jones. I'm here on behalf of Gabaldon Entertainment. Nice to meet you."

Darla just kept her eyes on her, not wanting to say a word.

The woman looked at the paper again, then brought her eyes back to Darla's.

"Say's here you're in for murder. Burnt down a rival's home." Lacy paused, but Darla didn't say a word. "Says here, there was a family in the basement apartment of the house you torched. The mother got out, but the children didn't. Burnt to a crisp."

"I didn't do it," Darla said, knowing what Lacy was already going to say. Everyone had said the same.

"Of course, you didn't."

"I was set up," Darla said, trying not to seem desperate with her plea. "Let me try to explain. My friend, June, she copied my work. A photograph that would display on Republic magazine. You get on that cover and your set. She took my photograph and claimed it as her own. I went to her house. We had a nasty fight about it. But while we fought we weren't alone. June's boyfriend Alex was there. Last thing I said was that I hope your career goes up in flames."

Darla paused, reflected, then continued. "I stormed out. But it was that night I got arrested. Cops came right to the door. I was told then what happened. But it wasn't me. Alex thought that June was cheating on her. He lit the flame." Darla paused again, reflected on her thoughts and her words. A moment passed and she continued.

"I know he did. I could never do such a thing. He put the gas canister he used in my car and the matches. I don't know how, but Alex did. That was who burnt the house down. He saw an opportunity and took it. Now those kids are gone and I'm the one they blame."

"Darla, I am not here to listen to a confession. I'm am here, though, to give you a solution to your problem."

Darla shifted in her seat. "My problem?"

Lacy smiled. "Yes, your lack of freedom. You're in for life, correct?"

"That's correct."

Lacy nodded. "What if I told you we could get you out sooner—much sooner. You could be free, raise your kids, run your business, have your life back."

Darla was hesitant at first with this woman, but Lacy had her attention now. "How so?"

Lacy smiled and glanced at the paper one more time. "Darla, have you heard of the show Dollhouse?"

Darla nodded. "Yeah, kinda, but—"

"You're not too sure what it is?"

"Yes."

"Yes, you do or yes, you—"

"Don't. I don't know anything about it. I've never seen it."

Lacy leaned in. "It's been going for 5 years now. It's been quite popular. Each episode lasts 10- 15 minutes. Premiering every second day with on average of 40-50 episodes a season. Each get over eight million views—more than any other program on the dark web."

"Congratulations," Darla said.

Lacy smiled at her sarcasm. "The game, Darla, is a way you can earn a reduced sentence with other perks. Can be a part of the special moments with your kids." Lacy had a gander at the paper. "Olivia and—"

"Luke."

"Luke, that's right. Cute kids. They survived the plague. You must be a proud mother."

"Always have been," Darla said sternly.

"Darla, I don't know if you're telling the truth about your crime—maybe you did it; maybe you didn't—but I'm here to offer you a chance. A life behind bars cut very short. Do this with us, and we'll grant you holidays with your family every year, and a reduced sentence, by giving you only seven more years of prison time. Does that sound like something that you'd be interested in?"

"Go on."

Lacy perused the papers again, then looked back at her, putting her hands together and lacing her fingers. "The premise of the show is to take prisoners, all with a crime related to children, and then wipe their current memory, only leaving it with the memories they had before their prison time and when the plague hit. It's a combination of a brain scan and a serum we inject you with. Sometimes, memories can pop through—our tools aren't always perfect. Are you okay with needles?"

Darla gave only a blank stare.

Lacy continued, "Once your memory's wiped, we place you in a house. One on an island just off the coast. In this house, you will wake up with six other prisoners who also had their memories erased. Millions will watch as your confused souls try and piece it all together. Trapped in a house that you'll be unable to get out of."

"What the hell?" Darla said in disgust.

"I'm not finished." Lacy smiled. "The house will be limited with resources, and you must complete challenges to earn these rewards. Once a day—at 6:00 pm or 9:00 pm, depending on your house—the door will open."

"Depending on the house?"

'We always have two houses to bounce back from. Keeps things fresh in case there are boring bits in-between each storyline. Anyway, back to the door. Once it's open, you'll have a chance to go outside. There, in the night, you'll have the option to leave. But this is where things get exciting. After the plague hit, Darla, we kept some infected individuals to use in our game. Releasing them at night, we let them hunt anyone who decides to leave."

Darla sat up, glaring in disbelief. "Why do this?"

"People are mad, Darla. Neighbours turned on one another when they were bitten. Families killed their own due to a disease that made their minds scramble; the average, good, tax-paying citizen was the prime target of a world on fire. Yet most prisoners—murders, thieves, rapists, and child killers like yourself—were safe and sound behind prison walls during all three months of madness. The people are angry, Darla. And now that the world's economy has hit an all-time low, keeping prisoners like you costs the world some serious dough. So, we wanted to both reduce the number of prisoners and have a way to make a profit. And this show brings in that money—and more satisfaction. Watching scum like you suffer is nothing but pure joy."

"So, you want me to be some contestant on your show. Be some kind of guinea pig for a disgusting society?"

"You're not one to judge."

"I didn't burn that house down. I didn't kill those kids.'

Lacy leaned back into her chair and crossed her arms. "Does it matter, Darla? You'll be rotting in jail for the rest of your prime years. A prison system that every single day will be watching your every move. You're living the Dollhouse life already. Why not play the game, earn a reduced sentence, and be with Olivia and Luke sooner rather than later."

Darla, with regret on her face, asked, "How do you win?"

"Ah, well, that's by being the last man standing. Or, eh, woman standing, if *you're* lucky. That's something new we're doing. One house with six women and one man, and the other with one woman and six men."

"Why?" Darla asked.

"Keeps things interesting. The theme for this year's season is the seven deadly sins. Each contestant has been jailed due to a crime related to the theme. So far, we have a gluttonous man named Lawrence who drunkenly cracked a kid's skull open last year. We also have Floyd, a man whose greed in 2026 made him poison his girlfriend to attempt to kill the baby inside her, which when he failed, he convinced his wife that it was food poisoning that made her so sick. 4 months later the baby was born, but Floyd suffocated his little girl in her crib, two weeks after she came home from the hospital. He tried to make it look as though it was an accident. But his lie was caught on tape. Little did he know his girlfriend bought a nanny cam that morning that he wasn't aware of, so his lie only lasted until the video was played. He did all that so he could simply save money to pay off a gambling debt."

"What monsters," Darla said, choked up.

"I'm not done. Another is Robert, a man who lusted after young girls. He was *never* fruitful, thank god. He was caught by his wife before he had the chance. He's been in prison for five years now. And now we want you, Darla—the woman who burnt down a friend's house who you envied, killing four small children in the process."

Darla began to sob. "I didn't do it. I swear."

Lacy smiled. "Most do believe you, Darla, but it doesn't matter if you did or not. The system sees you as guilty. And now your only quick way out is to play the game. Play the game until the last person is alive. It will go until then. Once there is only one person standing, the game is over. You've been through so much. Says here, March was quite the eventful month for you. Your husband died of cancer, you burned your rival's house down, and found out you were pregnant while in prison, only to have a miscarriage. Now, that is a crazy series of events. Is it really true?"

Darla nodded yes, wiping away her tears with her cuffed hands.

Lacy smiled. "Take this plunge, Darla. Look at the positives. For a moment's time, you'll forget, at least, about the arrest and prison sentence, the miscarriage, the plague, and yo —"

"Dyab!" Darla shouted in Creole, the word meaning Devil.

Lacy paused, kept her smile, then leaned back into her seat. "Okay, I don't know what that means. But let's continue. Most of these scum bags, we promise them their freedom, but we end up feeding them to the infected regardless. But you, Darla, your case seems different. The people who know your story well believe you're innocent. So, we'll keep our promise of what we have to offer to you. Play the game, Darla. Reduce your sentence, live your life, run your business again, and be with your children. Watch them grow up and rebuild this world that has been broken. Be there for them. Do it, Darla, for those two kids of yours."

Lacy slid the clipboard over to her with a pen. Darla glared at it, pondering on the choice that she had to make. Swallowing some courage, she took the pen, read over the document, and then, with her shaky hand, she signed the paper.

47

"I'm so sorry, Darla," Floyd said again as he stood behind, watching her.

Darla stumbled down the steps and went for the red door. Twisting the knob, Darla heard the door click, opening it. Floyd clasped onto her hair and pulled her away, tossing her to the back wall. He walked over, knife in hand and stuck her again in the same spot, this time not nearly as deep. Darla pushed against him, stepping away from the wall.

Her pain was unbearable. Grabbing hold of his wrist, Darla did all she could to pull the blade out of her, but Floyd steered her towards the wall again. Once there, Floyd pushed his weight against her, pressing her back against the wall. "God, I'm so sorry. Please forgive me. I'm so sorry," Floyd begged, but Darla wasn't able to speak. Blood spilled out of her gut and made its way down the blade and both her and Floyd's hand. As the blood trickled, Darla's hand started slipping. She couldn't keep a grip around his wrist. But when she finally moved, Floyd was able to push the blade in just a bit deeper.

With her other hand, Darla grabbed onto the back of Floyd's hair and squeezed it tight. With all her remaining strength, she pulled on every root she could for dear life. Floyd's head was forced back, and he screamed. So did Darla. Then, leaning forward, she bit down as hard as she could on his neck. Floyd couldn't take the pain and let go to push her back. When he did, Darla fell to the ground with the blade still in her.

With his right hand, Floyd rubbed the part of his neck that she'd bitten. "I deserve it, I know!" he cried out. He then grabbed onto her left ankle with his only working hand and began to try and pull her toward the door. As he was doing so, Darla pulled the blade out of herself; she screamed as it slipped out. Floyd dragged her past the door, and as they made it outside, Floyd let go of her and stepped over Darla, making his way back in. As he stepped past, with quick thinking, Darla stabbed him in his left leg, and Floyd toppled over. Using all the strength that she could muster, Darla dragged herself back inside as Floyd pulled the blade out.

As he did so, she got on top of him, trying to stop him from pulling out the knife. Luckily, she had the advantage of having two good hands. She then wrapped her hands around his neck. For a moment, she was able to squeeze, but that moment didn't last long enough. Floyd stuck his fingers into the wound on her stomach, and after that, Darla could only last a few seconds. She fell over to her side, then rolled onto her back.

"Floyd, please," she said with a weak breath.

But all Floyd did was pull the blade out of his leg, then got onto his knees to plunge the knife into Darla again. But before he was able to so, Darla kicked Floyd in the stomach, causing him to let go of the blade and stumble back, the knife hitting the wall and falling to the floor, toppling down to the second step of the basement staircase. During this, Darla got herself up, then she pushed Floyd outside and tried shutting the door.

Floyd stopped her from doing so by a hair. Both pushed against one another from the opposite sides of the door. Floyd, with an ounce more strength, was able to push through, and Darla landed on her back beside the steps leading downstairs. Floyd got on top of her, pinning her with his left arm, and with his right hand, he squeezed her throat as tightly as possible.

"Just l-let...it happen. Just let it fucking happen," Floyd said, begging her to die.

Darla, with no breath, was just able to see the knife as it teetered on the edge of the second step of the basement staircase. With just enough room, she was able to reach out and try to grab hold of it. But she was only able to touch the handle of the blade with the tips of her fingers. The more she felt it, the more it tilted and threatened to tumble down. Any sudden movements, jolts, any major shift in the body would cause the knife to fall down the steps. And then it would be game over.

As Floyd squeezed tighter, he cried out, saying, "It'll all be over soon. I'm sorry, Darla, I'm so sorry."

Darla could feel herself losing her motor functions. The lack of oxygen and the extreme blood loss was apparent. Looking up at Floyd, she could only see him as a silhouette due to the darkness around his image. His voice became softer, more muffled. It slowly began to go away, to the point where Darla only heard her heartbeat.

THUMP, THUMP, THUMP, THUMP. THUMP…THUMP…THUMP…THUMP…THUMP…

Darla regained her sense of touch and felt the handle of the knife in her hand.

THUMP…THUMP…THUMP…THUMP.

She saw Olivia and Luke playing in the backyard with her husband Evan, smiling and laughing.

THUMP…

THUMP…

THUMP…

It was then silent. Darla only saw her beautiful babies, sitting on the grass together, looking at her, smiling.

THUMP…

THUMP...

THUMP...

THUMP...

Silence.

Olivia and Luke turned to look at her, sitting next to one another on the grass, with the vision beginning to fade to darkness.

"We love you, Mommy," Olivia said.

Luke smiled, saying in his soft, caring voice, "We love you, Mommy. Come home. Please...come home. "

Darla got hold of the handle of the knife, swung the blade, and struck Floyd in the side of his ribcage. His right hand unclasped from her neck, and he let out a cry of searing pain as all her senses rushed back.

Opening her eyes, Darla grabbed hold of the knife and pulled it out of him. Floyd let out another scream, this time leaning forward. When he did, Darla swung the blade again, meaning to slash his throat but instead, she sliced open his left eye and partly cut his right.

Floyd's head snapped back, and he fell to the ground. "Aahhhhh, fuck!" he cried out.

Darla, trembling, stumbled as she got herself to her feet. Floyd reached over to her, trying to grab onto her leg, but Darla struck the knife into his right hand, then pulled it out straight after.

Pushing himself up, Floyd was now back on his knees. He was woozy, with two curled up and ruined hands and blood seeping from his eyes. Darla took a step back, and with all her might, she stabbed Floyd in the stomach.

Floyd let out a gasp as Darla screamed.

Standing up, Darla drove a kick that launched Floyd onto his back, straight out onto the porch. Raising his head, Floyd, battered and bloody, reached his left mangled hand out at Darla, looking for one last chance at possible forgiveness, but without hesitation, Darla stumbled to the door, clasped onto the handle, and forced it shut. The lock slid sideways, doing what it did best.

Darla slumped down to the floor, leaning her back against the red door.

A fist smacked against the glass, and as she leaned over, Darla saw Floyd on his knees with his bloody eyes, limp hands, cut leg, and the knife resting in his stomach. Leaning his bloody, sweating head against the window, Floyd begged for his life. "Please, let me win. My mother, Darla, she's sick. She needs me. Darla, please." Floyd sobbed uncontrollably now.

Darla turned her head away, ignoring his pleas. Again and again, he kept slamming his mangled fists against the window. "J-Jesus, Darla, don't do this, please. Don't do this!" Darla looked back at the desperate man for the last time, then began to get up. As he saw her leave, Floyd begged even more. "You have to let me win. Darla! I can't lose, Darla ... Fuck, don't do this. Where are you going. Stop! I beg you, let me win, Darla…. FUCK!"

Stumbling and holding onto the railing of the steps leading to the upper level, Darla, a hand on her stomach wound, and feeling the blood trickle between her fingers, took one last look at Floyd, then made her way up the steps. A wave of sudden exhaustion brought her to her knees, and she momentarily dropped to the floor before she pulled herself up against the wall.

Below, Floyd kept begging for her forgiveness, and his cries sank into her mind. "It's almost over now," Darla said to herself. Gripping her wound tightly, Darla, heavy-eyed, took a slow, relaxed breath.

Darla spoke words for her own comfort. "The woods are lovely dark and deep."

Floyd stopped looking through the window and stumbled his way off the porch. His strength was no longer there. He stumbled drunkenly to his knees, feeling weaker by the second. Looking at his stomach, he saw the knife that had been stuck in him. Floyd attempted to pull out the knife in his stomach with his limp hands, but, to no surprise, he wasn't able. "Come on, fucking… fucking bullshit," he mumbled to himself.

Darla took another breath. "But I have promises to keep."

She sat herself up and then slowly pulled off her cardigan, laying it out flat before wrapping it the best she could around her bleeding stomach.

Floyd looked up into the night sky, crying, terrified for his life. "Fuck... Fucking...shit. I won. I fucking won. She's dead. I won!" he cried out into the night sky, but only silence came in return.

Darla tied the cardigan into a tight knot and winced in pain as she did so. Through all of it, Darla kept the thought of Luke and Olivia in her mind, giving her a sense of calm. She saw their faces, felt their hugs, and heard their voices. Darla knew it was going to be okay.

Shutting her eyes, with another breath, she whispered, "And miles to go before I sleep." Darla exhaled, then smiled, muscling the strength to complete the final verse.

Floyd heard a rustling in the distance. There was a moment of silence with only the breeze and the clattering of branches, then the laughter of a small child sounded. He was looking out towards the deep, dark woods. Floyd saw the three of them—mother, daughter, and now Martin—walking towards him beginning to circle their prey. Floyd lifted his head with tears flowing, "Please, stop, stop. I won. I-I won. It's not fair, this isn't fair. Stop. Stop it. Please stop."

His sob's deepened, and with the sight he had left, Floyd saw the three of them, with casual stride and gleaming smiles, close in on him. His words were faint when he spoke, "No, no, no… No… No… stop… Stop, please…" The little girl turned and glanced at Martin, then her mother. The mother watched as the little girl stepped towards Floyd. His bleeding eyes catching hers. The little girl then stopped; her face went cold. She tilted her head as her yellow eyes glazed over, watching Floyd plead for his life. She then grew a smile of pure delight.

Darla, with just enough strength, opened her eyes and watched the clock. It went from reading 9:17, to the minute and second-hand snapping to the 12. A soft winter flake had begun, sticking and melting as it peppered the window. Her attention caught the snow, and she felt a sense of peace watching it come down. Darla smiled, and with the subtle strength that remained, the last line escaped her.

"And…miles to go…before…I sleep."

THE END

A massive thank you to all of those who took the time to read this book. I hope you enjoyed it and if you did, please leave a review. It helps indie authors out a great deal. Stay tuned; more thrills and chills to come. Take care.

-Andrew McManaman

Website: popcornpaperbacks.com

Email: andrew@popcornpaperbacks.com

Credits

Novel By
Andrew McManaman

Edited By
Paul Martin

Cover Art
Meg Rhoads

Book Blurb
Andrew Warren

Author Photo
Helen Burt

Book Trailer
Helen Burt
Anna Dziczkaniece

Beta Readers
Adam Moore
Anna Dziczkaniece
Anne Walsh
Bryony Dique
Cody Helem
Felicia Falcone

Hannah Stock

Holly Bune

Helen Burt

Jo Jasper

Jim McManaman

Meghalee Mitra

Rachel Silver

Sarah Haley

Vincent Walsh

ABOUT THE AUTHOR

Andrew McManaman was born in Ottawa and raised in the small rural community of Kemptville, Ontario, Canada. Being an avid reader and film buff, Andrew fell in love with storytelling right from a young age. Introduced to many badass classics growing up, he took a shine to the horror and thriller genre. At ten years old, Andrew wrote his first short story and fell in love with the act of writing and has kept writing ever since. Still to this day, a huge movie and book geek, many of the films he grew up watching are his true inspiration for his work. With Popcorn Paperbacks, his goal is to meld the genres he loved to watch growing up and his passion for writing together.